Symons, Julian
The Name of Annabel Lee

THE
NAME OF
ANNABEL
LEE

THE
NAME OF
ANNABEL
LEE

JULIAN SYMONS

THE VIKING PRESS   NEW YORK

Library of Congress Cataloging in Publication Data
Symons, Julian, 1912–
The name of Annabel Lee.
I. Title.
PR6037.Y5N27   1983   823'.912   83-47868
ISBN 0-670-34126-6

Grateful acknowledgment is made to Oxford University Press, Inc.,
for permission to reprint a selection from *Collected Poems*, by Conrad Aiken.
Copyright © 1953, 1970 by Conrad Aiken; renewed 1981 by Mary Aiken.

Printed in the United States of America
Set in Plantin

For Harald and Kirsten Mogensen

It was many and many a year ago,
    In a kingdom by the sea,
That a maiden there lived whom you may know
    By the name of Annabel Lee.
And this maiden she lived with no other thought
    Than to love and be loved by me.

She was a child and *I* was a child
    In this kingdom by the sea:
But we loved with a love that was more than love —
    I and my Annabel Lee,
With a love that the winged seraphs of heaven
    Coveted her and me.

And this was the reason that, long ago,
    In this kingdom by the sea,
A wind blew out of a cloud, chilling
    My beautiful Annabel Lee . . .

                    Annabel Lee, Edgar Allan Poe

Remember how you took the harlot's hand
And saw one instant hell's dark hinterland.

                    Conrad Aiken

Contents

PART ONE

1 *The Missing Link*

In literal truth each of us has only one life to live, one death to die, yet there is a sense in which it could be said that Annabel Lee died twice. So at least Dudley Potter always thought. He had nothing to do with her first death, but believed afterwards that his obsession with her was responsible for the second. Whether or not the belief was true is the subject of this story.

At the time they met Dudley Ernest Potter was thirty-nine years old, and unmarried. He had been born and brought up in Sussex, but came to the United States when he was twenty-four, to take a job as Assistant Professor in the English Department of Graham College. He had been there ever since, for several years now as a full Professor. His speciality was the minor Caroline poets, about whom he had published a number of articles in magazines edited, written and read by academics, and sponsored by University presses. Few students, however, wish to read deeply in John Cleveland, Shakerley Marmion or Henry King, and Dudley of necessity widened his teaching range. He taught a popular course on the Lake poets, and an even more successful one on Poe and Whitman, varying these with a course on nineteenth century English novelists from George Eliot onwards. He had, in a small way, a reputation in the world outside Graham as the man who knew about the Caroline poets. Not many people know much about the Caroline poets.

Graham has about four thousand students, and is a pretty good private college. It is in lush exurbia, halfway between New Haven and New York, an hour's drive from the Big Apple. Most of the students come from well-to-do Eastern families, whose sons and daughters have not quite qualified for top Ivy League schools, yet although Graham knows itself to be second-best it is far from second-rate. 'We do not pretend to be very high-powered,' Dexter Norman, the

President, would say, with a whimsical smile suggesting that the absence of nationally famous names on the Graham faculty was a positive virtue. 'We simply aim to turn out complete men and women.'

Dudley disliked all of his own names. The first was perhaps just all right, but from his schooldays onwards he had been called "Dud", and an abbreviation acceptable enough for Dudley Moore inevitably jarred on a scholar who had become an academic. Ernest was unbearable, and Potter had a regrettable crudeness. It was the combination of *Dudley* with *Potter*, however, that seemed overwhelmingly dull, and at times he felt the dullness to be justified. A full-length glass, however, showed nothing much wrong. He was two inches under six feet, and swimming and tennis kept his figure in reasonable trim. The face was pale, roundish, the eyes blue, the carefullybrushed hair changing from its original mouse to a rather becoming grey. So what *was* wrong? The face in the glass regarded him with the wary, withdrawn look of somebody who expects the worst to happen, and although he deplored this expression he knew it to be characteristic.

Shy, withdrawn, hopelessly commonplace, those would have been his condemnatory words about himself. Yet like many shy people he was capable of splendidly witty thoughts, although these thoughts rarely came through in memorable utterances. In optimistic moods he felt himself to be an ironical, detached observer of life, even though he was aware of a longing to be participant rather than observer. He knew that he had a reputation among the faculty and students for an aloofness which he rather cultivated, feeling that it was in tune with ironical detachment.

All this was before he met Annabel Lee.

On a warmish November evening Dudley cooked himself a mushroom omelette, and then strolled down from the Hospitality Residences where he lived to the J. G. O'Neill Drama Hall. The Residences were a small block of ten apartments used to house visiting lecturers, and other guests who needed temporary accommodation on campus. They had a living room, one large and another smallish bedroom, and a neat well-fitted kitchen. Dudley had been put into one of these apartments when he first arrived, and had successfully resisted attempts to move him to one of the blocks occupied by students plus a few of the faculty, or into a family that would have provided him with meals. He had felt at first that he could not bear to have any close contact with other people, and what had begun as a reaction to the emotional catastrophe that made him leave England, had developed into habit. For a while successive Deans of Residence had insisted that the arrangement was not permanent, but it had been sanctified by time.

The Drama Hall, a name for some reason thought preferable to theatre, was five minutes' walk away in one of the pleasantest parts of the campus, removed from the student blocks and with a view of the tennis courts. J. G. O'Neill, who gave the Hall to Graham, was a millionaire truck owner whose copybook had been smudged, although not completely blotted, by allegations that he had a financial arrangement with Jimmy Hoffa through which he was able to keep down his drivers' wages. The Drama Hall, a squat red-brick building, was an acknowledgement of the fact that Graham had accepted a couple of young O'Neills at a time when J.G. was under investigation by a Congressional Committee.

Drama, particularly of the avant-garde kind, was one of the things for which Graham was best known. Elinor Cruise, the director of drama, was a large woman who wore flowing shapeless dresses, and had a mass of hair which was sometimes piled on top of her head and at other times dropped beneath her shoulders in a slightly tangled reddish-gold mass. She had once been assistant producer to a man who claimed to have worked with a protégé of Gordon Craig, and she laid much stress on originality and modernity. Elinor was responsible for all the Drama Hall productions. Although some classical works were inevitable, she tried to avoid everything between Euripides and Brecht, and her particular feeling was for small modern companies who performed largely extemporised work. When such companies visited Graham, Elinor made it plain that she would regard it as some kind of betrayal if the arts department was poorly represented in the audience.

There were, nevertheless, many absentees. Dudley would have been among them if Elinor had not caught him one day in the faculty restaurant. There was between them the link of what she occasionally referred to as *that evening*. On *that evening* Dudley had drunk a good deal at a faculty party, and perhaps Elinor also had taken on more liquor than her large frame generally absorbed. They had argued about something ridiculous and of which he knew nothing, Brecht's work pre- and post-war perhaps, and in the flush of argument Elinor's powerful shoulders, formidable breasts and cascading hair had seemed immensely attractive. Presumably the attraction had existed for her also. There had, anyway, been a session in her apartment which he had as nearly as possible obliterated from his mind. Neither of them had made any gesture towards repeating it, but *that evening* always — or so he felt — hovered in the air, a kind of threat or promise. Because of it he was always particularly polite to Elinor.

'Thursday evening, Dud. What are you doing?' Her voice was rich, deep, theatrically thrilling. The correct reply was to plead immediately a visit to New York or a dinner engagement. Instead he hesitated, fatally. "The Missing Link", she said triumphantly.

'What's that?'

'*What's that*? The most original company I've seen in twenty years, my dear, that's all. A new conception of drama.'

'An Off Broadway company?'

'*Off Broadway,*' Elinor gave the impression that had a spittoon been handy she would have used it. Her natural colour heightened. 'Gene Beecham wouldn't look at Off Broadway, or Off Off Broadway for that matter. This is total theatre, you've got to experience it.'

He said weakly, 'I'm not sure I shall like them.'

'Like them, hate them, what does it matter? You must *experience* them. The show runs three nights but I shall expect you on Thursday. I'll send a ticket.'

He could have wriggled out of Thursday, but what would have been the use? It would have been Friday or Saturday. Once caught by Elinor the only thing, at least for somebody with *that evening* and the threat of its repetition hanging over him, was submission.

He entered the Hall, which was already two-thirds full, hoping to be able to slip unnoticed into a seat and perhaps escape at the interval. An usher whom he recognised as a girl who had registered for one of his classes and left it after a week on the ground that it was unenterprising, looked at the ticket and said, 'Down the left aisle. Elinor's waiting for you.'

And indeed Elinor moved upon him, resplendent in a mauve gown with long purple earrings, hair piled unbelievably high, breath strongly but ambiguously scented. Her hand on his arm was vice-like.

'There you are, Dud. We've been waiting.' He said that he could sit anywhere. 'Didn't you look at the ticket? Faculty members are part of our participating audience.'

Of course he had not looked closely at the ticket, and now it was too late. Still with that policeman's grip she led him to the stage, which had been divided into several cubicles all visible from the auditorium. In the biggest of them, which seemed to represent an office, he found himself in the presence of two other faculty members. Edna Molony was a fierce young woman who taught a course on structuralism, and another called "Woman Power in Literature". Beside her was Denny Marston, a sociologist who prided himself on looking like a student, and often tried to act like one. The student audience cheered as Dudley was seen on the stage. Denny clasped his hands over his head like a boxer, and indicated that Dudley should do the same. Instead, too cowardly to leave the stage onto which he had been lured, he folded his arms and tried to appear resigned, although he knew that the effect was often to suggest superciliousness.

A man strolled on from the wings and said, 'Hi. I'm Gene Beecham.'

Gene Beecham was a squat man, with eyebrows that met in the middle and a Zapata moustache. He wore a peaked cap, and a uniform with several flashes on it that said "SS", "CIA" and "KGB", along with less familiar conjunctions of letters. The Missing Link, he said, was the one between guilt and innocence. His voice sounded like gravel being dragged over asphalt.

'We're gonna show you an interrogation set up, and what we're sayin' is everything goes on at the same time, so if you're talkin' about one pig you're talkin' about 'em all, if you're showin' the 87th Precinct you're showin' Vietnam and the Lubianka, the way it is for blacks is the same way it is for browns and yellers and poor whites. At the same time we got no bias, what we're saying is who's innocent, who's guilty, ain't the right questions, it's the state of the nation and the state of the world we're showin' you tonight.'

There was a good deal more of the same, decorated by expletives that always made Dudley feel uncomfortable when they were uttered in public. Should he get up and go? To do so would make him appear conspicuous, and before he could make a decision the cast, four other men and two women, had appeared in that surreptitious way characteristic of modern drama, and the action had begun.

It proceeded simultaneously in the different cubicles. In one, painted to look like a cell, a woman screamed as a man in uniform pretended to beat her up, in another a man sat with his feet on the table drinking whisky. In the main office Beecham, behind his desk, interrogated Edna and Denny about their links with somebody named Bateman, who was said to have played a part in the Bay of Pigs and in Kennedy's assassination. Edna's denials were shrill, and Beecham came round his desk and appeared to grab her by the hair. Edna responded with a fine feminist blow to the solar plexus. The students roared approval.

The roar decided Dudley. He got up to leave the stage. One of the two uniformed guards beside Beecham came over and caught him by the arm.

'Where you think you're going?'

'I've had enough of this nonsense.'

'You're not leaving, Mr —'

'Potter. Yes, I am. Let go of me.'

'Potter, is it? We wanna talk to you, Potter. Here.'

He found himself pushed into the cubicle next to Beecham's office. A woman said, 'Sit down.'

It was characteristic of Dudley that at this moment

several possible courses of action occurred to him. He could leave, and if his departure was resisted could try an Edna-blow at the young thug, who was a couple of inches shorter than himself. He could step to the front of the stage and denounce the whole thing as rubbish. He could put a foot or a fist through one of the frail partitions separating the cubicles. But all of these things would have exposed him to the ridicule or hostility of the students, and he did none of them. He sat down.

The woman opposite him, who sat at a much smaller desk than Beecham's, wore a dark blue jacket, trousers of a mock-military kind, knee-high boots and a cap set jauntily to one side. She pushed a number of photographs across the desk and said sharply, in a mid-Atlantic accent: 'Look at these. See if you recognise anybody.'

He said no, although in fact he did recognise photographs of several film stars and statesmen. She leaned forward.

'There was a picture of JFK in that pile. You mean to say you didn't recognise him?'

'Of course I did. I thought you meant —'

'Don't think, Potter, you're not here to think. And don't play games. You know half-a-dozen of the people in those pictures, don't you?'

'Yes.'

'And Bateman, what about Bateman?'

To one side he heard Beecham shouting, on the other the woman suffering a mock beating-up was crying, 'Mercy, oh have mercy.' The phrase woke the memory of his father, his mother, the abolished past. He felt himself trembling with anger, and also on the brink of tears. He stood up and said, in a voice not quite steady: 'I've had enough. I'm leaving.'

The uniformed guard moved forward, but the woman held up a hand. 'Okay, Mr Potter is clear, he has no connection with Bateman. Thanks for your co-operation, Mr Potter.' In a lowered voice, with the suggestion of a smile, she said, 'I don't blame you.'

That was when he noticed her for the first time, the full mouth, the small ears flat against the head, the light blue eyes set wide apart.

As he walked off the stage he heard Denny shouting: 'Yes, I admit it, I knew Bateman at the Bay of Pigs, I was one of the agents he used to frame Oswald.' The last sound that came to him as he left the Drama Hall was the clapping hands of the students.

Then he was out in that unsuitably mild November night, walking back home. Voices were raised in laughter from the student blocks at the right. On the left the lights of the library showed and a single figure could be seen going up the steps. He walked to the library, feeling that buried in his carrel there he might blot out the memories jangling in his mind like discordant bells. Then he turned away at the very door. The images of his father, his mother, Elaine, were clear in his head as they had not been for years.

That night he slept little, but he did not think about the girl who had sat opposite him on the stage. Nor was she in his mind on Friday morning when he taught his course on what, that semester, was called mid-Victorian poetry, in which Tennyson and Arnold, Clough and Coventry Patmore, provided a change from the Lake poets. His presentiment that something disturbing was about to happen was temporarily checked by awareness that some of the class were waiting the chance to make a joke about the previous night. It came when somebody asked whether he thought Clough provided a link between Tennyson and Arnold. A voice said audibly, "The missing link," and a little ripple of laughter became a roar when he said: 'That is an extremely feeble joke.' He could not identify the voice, and in any case what could he have done without making himself look more foolish? Any news involving the discomfiture of a faculty member spread like mercury through Graham, and the sensible thing to do was to leave it alone.

He left it alone, but when the morning was over felt unable to face the jokes and mock-sympathy that would greet him in the faculty restaurant, and went to Peter's Place downtown. In fifteen years he had not become reconciled to American fast food, and ate a hamburger or a pizza only when they were inescapable, at a party, a barbecue or cook-out. He ordered a ham and swiss cheese sandwich on rye, and settled down with a book in one of the cubicles. He was making notes when a voice asked: 'Is it all right if I sit here?' It was the girl from the Drama Hall. There was only one possible answer, and he made it.

She was wearing a striped shirt and light grey skirt that made her look a different person from the peremptory figure behind the desk. 'You hated last night, didn't you?'

'It was preposterous nonsense.' Feeling that there might have been something shrill in his voice he added, 'I don't mean anything personal.'

'Never mind. Why did you let that awful woman get you on to the stage?'

'You don't know Elinor. And she hadn't told me what was going to happen. Yes, I hated it. Thank you for helping to rescue me.'

'You either love it or loathe it, being part of the action I mean. Your friend, what's his name, loved it.'

'Denny Marston. But he's not my friend. He's in social science.'

'He ended up admitting he was in a group called KAP, short for Kill All Presidents.' She bit into a sandwich with vigour.

'I don't think that's funny.'

'Gene went wild about him, the students loved it, how come you're so stuffy?'

'Is it being stuffy not to find the murder of Presidents funny? Then put me down as having no sense of humour.' She looked at him, and for a moment he thought she was going to say that was just what she did think. He shook his head and laughed. 'Stupid remark. Sorry. Last night upset me more than it should have done. But surely you don't find the idea of murder funny?'

'I think everything's funny.' He shook his head. 'Skip it. What are you reading?' When he held up the book she asked, 'Who's John Cleveland?'

'He was a seventeenth century poet, a Royalist who supported King Charles. He lost a Cambridge fellowship and went to prison because of it. A lot of poems are attributed to him which weren't really his.'

'And so? Should you care?'

'It may seem silly, but yes, I do. I've been working for

21

years on a definitive edition that will include all the genuine poems. I shall be talking about him and some other poets of the same period to my class this afternoon.'

She said nothing, but the glance she gave him was full of mockery. At that moment he was first aware of her as a sexually attractive woman and felt a current of desire flowing between them. It was in his mind to tell her something more about Cleveland, to say that textual examination of the poems had become almost a nightly ritual for him, but he refrained. She would think such a nightly occupation absurd, and he did not wish her to think him absurd.

'What's your name?' He hesitated. 'I'll tell you mine. Irma Grese.'

'But that's —'

'The Bitch of Belsen, I know. It's what Gene calls me. He says I should think myself into Irma's mentality as an interrogator. I went soft last night, didn't I?'

'What revolting nonsense.'

'If you say so. I told you, for me anything goes. But Gene now, he's on an ego trip all the time, it's getting to be a bore. I think I've just about had Gene. Smoke?' He shook his head. She lighted a cigarette. 'My real name's ridiculous. Annabel Lee. Yes, Annabel Lee as in the poem by Poe, that's what people always say. Annabel Lee Fetherby. My mother was nuts about Poe.'

'I don't think your name is ridiculous. It's charming. My name, now—'. He gulped, then managed to say it. 'Is Dudley Potter. I detest it.'

She considered. 'I can see you might. No middle name?'

'Ernest.' She made a face. 'People call me Dud.'

'And you don't like that? No, I suppose not. I get called Ann or Annie, except when people use my full name as a put-down, or some kind of crummy joke. Let's both be Lee, what do you say? And Lee, may I come to your class this afternoon?'

'What for?'

She mimicked him. 'What for, what for, why do you have to ask? Let's say I'm interested.'

'I can't believe that.'

'You do put yourself down, don't you?' she cried, almost

in admiration. 'All right, say I'm bored with Gene and these stupid kids who think he's a genius, say Graham's not exactly a metropolis and there's nothing else to do, say I want to know what goes on in a course about a poet I've never heard of, say I want to learn something. Just don't say *what for*.'

He looked at her across the table, and thought: why do you bother with me? He thought also: why should I feel the slightest wish to impress somebody who uses the slang clichés of the time, who talks about ego trips and putting yourself down? 'It's called auditing the course,' he said.

'All right, then, can I audit the course?'

There were only half-a-dozen students taking the minor Carolines. The hour was spent examining the conceits in William Hammond's *To His Scornful Mistress* and Cleveland's *To the State of Love*. He was very much aware of Annabel Lee's presence and of her glances moving between him and the students but, strangely, this made him more fluent than usual. He was conscious of a rare eloquence as he impressed on them the genuineness behind Cleveland's conceits. When it was over she walked back with him to the Residences, and he realised with a shock of surprise that she was staying in them.

'Where are you?' She pointed to an apartment two doors from him. 'Well, goodbye. Now you can see what a dull life we live at Graham.'

He removed his glove, took her hand. Her face, framed in the hood of the parka she wore, seemed to be overflowing with laughter.

'Oh, come *on*, Lee,' she said.

That was how it began.

That was Friday afternoon. On that night she took her part in the Missing Link charade, then returned to his apartment. He knew that the last performance was on Saturday and that the company would return to New York that night. At six in the evening she said that she must get ready.

'It's goodbye, then,' he said awkwardly. She stood there smiling at him. He would have liked to think the smile was enigmatic, Sphinx-like, but it was more nearly the smile of a young girl playing some joke understood by nobody but herself. 'And thank you.'

Oh, this is terrible, he thought, I might be giving thanks for tea or dinner. 'I don't know what to say. Nothing like this has happened to me before.' It had certainly been nothing like *that evening*.

She still said nothing, but lightly kissed his cheek. Then she was gone, leaving him uncertain of his feelings. Self-analysis came naturally to him, and now he tried to separate his wonder at what had happened from the pleasure he had enjoyed. There was a certain uneasy, old-fogeyish feeling that her presence in his apartment even for so short a time had disturbed the pattern of his life. She had insisted on a boiled egg at breakfast, for instance, so he had boiled one for himself as well. He had also eaten four instead of two pieces of toast. 'What thoughts for a great lover,' he reflected, and regarded himself in the glass, pale face, worried look, touches of grey hair, and thought how ludicrous was the idea of Dudley Potter as any sort of lover. 'It's over now,' he told the figure in the glass, and settled down determinedly to mark some essays. He had so far forgotten her that when the bell rang he thought it must be a student, even though the time was eleven o'clock. She stood there, a small suitcase in her hand.

'I thought you were going to New York.'

'You look as if you wish I had.' She came in, put down

the suitcase. 'I've come to stay. If you want me, that is.' He said something about Beecham, and about leaving the company. 'It's the way you said, they're a lot of pseuds. I'd only been with them three weeks. As for Gene he's so drugged up he doesn't know whether he's on the stage or in the Lubianka half the time. I've had him up to here.' She touched her neck. 'I'm a butterfly, Lee, and I've landed on you. Aren't you pleased?'

The twelve weeks that followed were the happiest of Dudley Potter's life, and indeed, looking back, it seemed to him that in her company he understood for the first time the full possibilities of living. In part, this was because he had never passed a night with a woman. Her few clothes hung in the wardrobe, her make-up and toilet things lay beside his in the bathroom, and this was so strange to him that he felt as though he were living through the events of a dream. Each time he put the key in the door he half expected to see the place as it had been before she came, restored to its usual tidiness with no cigarette stubs in the ashtrays, no towel left on the bathroom floor or blonde hairs in the bath. She was untidy, academically ignorant, often used words and phrases that jarred on him. None of these things was of the least importance.

Perhaps in every love affair there is an element of obsession. It was strongly present in Dudley's case, probably because he lacked much sensual experience. Although he had performed the sexual act in his fifteen years at Graham, it had always — even or especially on *that evening* — been without thought of the other person involved. There were times when he had felt almost desperately the need of a partner to whom he could confide thoughts and aspirations. He went so far as to put an advertisement in the personals column of the *New York Review of Books*, among those that began *Handsome sophisticated male, 34, seeks woman of wit and experience . . . Elegant classy dame, turned on by Tolkien and Woody Allen, searches for humanist humorous male . . .* The results had varied from the ludicrous to the dismaying.

In the presence of Annabel Lee (which was how he always thought of her, although he mostly brought himself to say only Lee) inhibitions were swept away. She seemed prepared to do and say anything, yet it would have been wrong to use a word like *shameless* about her. It was rather that, as she had said that first day at lunch in Peter's Place, she found everything comic, so that sex like anything else was a kind of game to be played enthusiastically. She was delighted by wind-breaking, eager that they should watch each other urinating, and always felt passionately hungry after the act, so that she would eat anything from a bar of chocolate to a ham sandwich, gulping it down as if she were starving. Sometimes she suggested variations on the act itself that shocked him.

'How do you know unless you try?' she asked, when he had refused one of these suggestions.

'I do know. I should detest it.'

'But suppose it gives me pleasure? All right, all right, don't look like a small boy refusing nasty medicine. I'm not complaining, we'll do something else.' She sat naked on the bed, legs crossed under her, and quoted:

'Never Mark Antony
Dallied more wantonly
With the fair Egyptian Queen.'

'Cleveland. You've been reading him.'

'Why not? He's all around here, and I wanted to see what had been occupying you all these years. He was a sexy fellow, your old John. Remember that poem you read to the students? You left out the best bit:

Then have at all, the pass is got,
For coming off, oh, name it not!
Who would not die upon the spot?

Do you feel that, Lee, would you like to die upon the spot? Sometimes you look like it. Or would you say: "Very pleasant, I've enjoyed it, but I'm afraid I have a class in ten minutes"?'

'What about you?'

'Oh, I'd do anything.' She held up a paper card of tablets. 'Supposing I said let's take a trip, would you do it?'

'Take a trip? Oh, you mean LSD. No, I shouldn't want to do that. I like to stay in control of what's happening.'

She made a face. 'Prissy.'

'Where did you get them?'

'Silly, they're not what you'd call drugs, just soother-downers. I sometimes need a soother-downer.'

He took her hand. 'There are things I don't want to do, perhaps because of the past.'

'What happened in the past?'

'I'll tell you one day. I love you, Annabel Lee.'

'Lee.'

'I love you, Lee.'

'I love Lee too. But does that mean we love ourselves or each other?'

He did not fail to notice that in this exchange she did not say she loved him, and indeed she never used the word. When he said that for her desire was not connected with love she did not deny it, nor did she contradict him when he said that anything was permissible to her because she took nothing seriously. At times there was something that almost frightened him in her attitude, but for the most part he was charmed by something wholly outside his past experience. She enjoyed the element of exaggeration and absurdity in Cleveland's poems, and one day quoted a line to him the moment he came in the door: "Why doth my she-advowson fly incumbency?" Don't look so surprised. I can read, though I had to look up advowson in the dictionary, and even then it took me five minutes to understand it. But I'm not flying incumbency, am I? You can have your advowson now, no waiting.'

These were sensual pleasures, but it was others that filled his heart. To return after taking a class, with twilight fading to darkness, and see a light gleaming in the living room window, gave him a feeling of joy known only to those who have lived alone. She had a passion for the literature of cooking, and brought home armfuls of books from the local bookstore. When he remonstrated mildly she told him that she had once written a cook book.

'You mean it was published?'

'If you knew how condescending you sound, Professor. Yes, it was published. *Cooking Through the Year* by Annabel Lee Fetherby, a recipe for every day of the year,

27

and one over for Leap Year.'

After that he said nothing further about her literary acquisitions. The actual dishes she made, her new way of cooking flounder, the special sauce for ham that she had discovered in a book of old Charleston recipes, did not seem to him to justify the pains spent on them, but perhaps that was often the way with cooks.

When he looked back on those twelve weeks he found that she had not told him much about herself. He was not by nature curious, and it did not occur to him to ask questions about her past, or about why it was that she never seemed to lack money. One day, however, he was passing Graham Post Office when she came out holding a letter. She opened it, then saw him across the street, greeted him with a smile in which there was something uneasy, and put the letter in her pocket. He would have felt it crudely impolite to ask whether she was having mail sent to her at the Post Office, but she forestalled any possible question.

'That was my allowance. It comes every quarter. I know what you're like, you'd be embarrassed to have mail addressed to me at your apartment, so I have it sent to the Post Office.'

It had seemed to him that she was reading a letter, but still he accepted what she said. When they got home, however, she talked about her family for the first time.

'My mother's name was Rose Scudamore. She was what you might call a lady.' She made a face. 'Cheltenham Ladies College, Somerville, her father was a Brigadier-General who did something unimportant in the War. So Rose was well brought up, but what did she do? Married a grocer from Yorkshire, became Mrs Horace Fetherby. Not a chain of groceries, just a single shop in Halifax. Which is where I was brought up, along with my sister, who was three years younger. Guess what she was called?' He shook his head. 'Lenore. Annabel Lee and Lenore, can you imagine? I told you mother was dotty about Poe. So there she was, Mrs Fetherby the grocer's wife, with Horace the grocer and her two kids with the ridiculous names. If you think Dudley's funny, you should try being called Annabel

28

Lee or Lenore at a local grammar school.'

'The Scudamore family had cut her off?'

'Not a bit of it. They were friendly as could be, it was Rose who didn't want anything to do with them because she said they were snobbish about Horace. She loved Horace.'

'And Horace made a fortune as a grocer and ended up Mayor of Halifax?'

'Wrong again. Horace's brother Stewart was the success, owns I don't know how many supermarkets. Our branch of the Fetherbys had nothing but catastrophes. First of all Lenore ran off to London when she was fifteen, was found and brought back, got done for shoplifting a year later, then sent to a girls' Borstal. Horace wrote a letter saying never darken my grocery counter again, she said the next time she saw any of us would be too soon. When she came out of the slammer we heard from her a couple of times though. She wrote from London saying she was working as a model, then that she had a boy friend who was doing a lot of deals with the Arabs and they were probably going to live in Saudi Arabia for a while. When Horace died we couldn't get in touch with her. Mother wrote, but the letter came back marked "Gone away".'

'You didn't know the boy friend's name?'

'Sure. It was Jones.' Her laughter was unaffected, joyful. 'Lenore heard somehow about Horace's death and wrote, once from Libya, the other time with a London postmark but no address.'

'Were you — are you — fond of her?'

She considered. 'I suppose, in a way. She was unstable. I am too, we got it from Rose. When we were trying to find her, Rose used to go around reciting that line about "The sweet Lenore hath gone before, with Hope, that flew beside", but I think she really enjoyed the drama and mystery.'

'What about your father?'

'Horace? He droped dead of a heart attack when he was serving some rashers of bacon to a customer. Died at his post, you might say. Then a couple of months later the Brigadier-General was banging along in his Rover, Mrs Brig by his side, sedate as can be according to witnesses, skidded on a patch of black ice, ran into a tree and — bingo, they're both kaput. She died at once, he on the way to hospital. So guess what, the whole Scudamore estate went to Rose. Of course taxes took a big slice, but there was more left than Horace or she had ever dreamed of. Mother had already sold the grocery shop to Stewart. Now she disposed of the Scudamore assets, bought a place on the Yorkshire coast and settled down to paint. You should see the pictures. Talk about Edgar Allan, they were weird. She died of cancer five years ago.'

'Were you living at home?'

'Me?' she echoed on a note of surprise. 'Not likely. I left at nineteen. Not home birds, the Fetherby girls. I took an acting course that was a waste of time, got into a little theatre company, took jobs as waitress and switchboard opeator, did a bit more acting here and there, wrote my cookbook and made some money out of that. No steady job, didn't want one. Then when mother died, she left the lot to me. Only in trust, mind. I get the interest, but can't touch the capital until I'm thirty, which will be in a few months.'

'You don't look thirty. Or anything like it.'

'Oh gallant Lee,' she said mockingly. 'Well, I am, or shall be next June. The interest is enough to keep me going, and very nice too. I'm not one of the world's workers by nature.'

'Why did you join that awful Missing Link company?'

'I like the stage. The Missing Link sounded like fun.' She gave him a sidelong glance to see his reaction. 'Gene and I had something going, or I thought so. I was wrong.'

He had never asked her, but he had known she must have slept with that squat loathsome figure. Yet in spite of the knowledge he felt a real physical pain, acute as indigestion, round the heart.

'What happened to Lenore?'

'Oh yes, Lenore, I forgot. She heard about mother's death somehow, turned up at the funeral. She said she'd been all over the Middle East, acting as personal assistant to various unnamed sheikhs. I suspect her of living what a good Graham academic might think of as a wicked life. And of being on her beam ends at the time, although I must say she looked all right. I think she came up to the funeral

30

hoping for a handout. If so she was unlucky.'

'You talk about them all as if they were strangers. Or enemies.'

'I'm not sentimental, if that's what you mean. Horace was a fool, Rose was a silly woman, slightly dotty, Lenore was a pretty fair bitch. I always thought so, and I've not changed my mind because they're dead. Are you sentimental about your mother and father? Are they still alive?'

He said with difficulty, 'My father, yes, I think so. My mother is dead.'

'An only child, of course. It shows, don't think it doesn't. What about those snaps under your shirts? No good looking like that, if you leave things around I shall look at them.'

She got out the little bunch of photographs and went through them, asking who's this, where was that taken? There were several of his father — bowling to him in the garden, a wooden box behind him for a wicket, standing in the doorway of "Woodlands", in the drive beside the car with his mother, waving a hand out of the car window. There were snaps of Dudley himself, in the school tennis team, dressed up as Henry the Eighth on a rag day, on holiday in Devon with Elaine and Steve Shilton. There were others with Elaine at "Woodlands", one with his mother and father, his arm round Elaine's shoulders, everybody smiling.

'She was a student I knew when I was at King's College, London. We were engaged to be married.'

'*Engaged*,' she said scornfully. 'But it didn't come off.'

'It didn't come off.'

'And who's this?'

'Steve Shilton. He was my closest friend. I haven't seen him for years, but we keep in touch.'

'Shilton?' She looked at the snap closely. 'What does he do now?'

'He's head of the family law firm, Shilton and Mallett, and a partner in some publishing outfit, which is what really interests him.'

She stopped him with a hoot of pleasure. 'He's *my* Shilton. I mean, the one who dishes out my allowance. I thought I recognised him. Tell him you met me when you write again, it'll be a kind of guarantee I'm being respectable. Not that he's exactly stuffy.'

'He was a bit wild at college. Not like me.'

'Not like you.' In her wide blue eyes he thought he saw for a moment something like contempt. Then she was gathering up the photographs, and laughing. She laughed a lot, always with evident enjoyment. As she put the snaps back in the drawer she said, 'All boring stuff, isn't it? I hate the past, wish it had never existed. I like to wipe the slate clean every year. That's the end of happy families, they don't belong to real life. Let's get back to she-advowsons and incumbency.'

The past still nagged at him, as he knew it would forever, yet the phrasing charmed him. And charmed, in the sense of bewitched, was what he felt himself to be. There was so much about her that he disapproved, her frequent coarseness of language and manner, the greediness with which she approached anything she enjoyed as though it were an orange from which she was intent to suck the last drop of sweetness, the hardness that was never far below the surface of her gaiety, and a sort of deliberate irresponsibility manifested in such things as her lack of clothes. She had only what she had brought in her single suitcase, a dress, a skirt, two pairs of jeans, a couple of sweaters, bras and pants and makeup, little more. Yet when he urged her to buy things in Graham she looked at him with her eyes wider than usual, and asked: 'Why?'

He said helplessly: 'Don't you want new clothes?'

'What for?'

'You have so few. If money is a problem —'

'I told you, I can look after myself moneywise. I travel light, that's all. Most people lumber themselves with a lot of rubbish.'

'You said you'd been with the Missing Link only a couple of weeks. I suppose the rest of your things are at home in England.'

'Home,' she said, as though uttering an unknown word, then nodded. 'I see what you mean. I used to keep a flat near Kennington Oval, nice dingy area. Gave it up a few months back. I was hardly ever in it.'

'So you've got no home?'

32

'Don't make it sound like a tragedy.' She watched him across the room. 'Lee.'

'Yes?'

'Remember what I said that first night about being a butterfly and landing on you? That's still the way it is.' When he did not reply, she let fly with a volley of abuse about his primness and the pettiness of the world in which he lived, a volley spotted with the four-letter words that she knew he disliked. Then she put on her parka and went out, slamming the door. A couple of hours later she returned, and said briefly that she was sorry.

That was a week before Christmas. He had feared that she might suddenly say she was going back to England, but Christmas found her in high spirits. She insisted on putting up decorations and that sort of thing, and cooked a turkey with two different stuffings, one with chestnuts, cornbread and fillet of veal, the other including among its ingredients cracker crumbs and sherry. At this meal they entertained Denny Marston and his wife Martha, and Willie and Mary Rushmore. Willie was the Dean of Faculty, a big bald pipe-smoking man, and Mary had a secretarial job on campus. The Rushmores had been kind to Dudley in his early days at Graham, and they passed for his closest friends, although that was not very close. They were a pleasant, honest, un-exciting couple, whose reactions on any subject were conventional, as Graham knew convention.

The fact that Dudley had a woman installed in his apart-ment had not passed unnoticed. The crudest reaction came from Denny, who literally slapped him on the back.

'So you're shacked up, Dud. Glad to hear you finally made it into real life. Feel ten years younger, I'll bet.'

It would have been difficult, he thought, to pack more insults into a sentence, but one could never feel sure that Denny meant to be rude. Of course not everybody was like Denny. Approval was generally expressed, in the form of smiles, nods, and remarks that Lee was a very pretty girl. At drink or dinner parties with the Pages, the Mortimers, and other people in the English department, Annabel Lee was uncharacteristically wary, not the outspoken girl Dudley knew. No doubt, he thought, she did not wish to shock his

33

friends. Things were different, however, on Christmas Day. As often happened, Annabel Lee's cooking ambitions were not altogether fulfilled in practice. The lyonnaise potatoes were slightly burnt, the veal in the chestnut stuffing not quite cooked. The Rushmores, as Dudley was uneasily aware, did not hit it off well with the Marstons. But still, a reasonably merry atmosphere was maintained, fuelled by New York State champagne and California burgundy, until Mary said that Annabel Lee was an unusual name.

'My mother was crazy about Edgar Allan Poe. I had a sister named Lenore, would you believe it?'

'Not really,' Denny said, and laughed as though he had made a joke.

'And my father was a grocer.' Annabel Lee laughed, as though this too were a joke.

Martha, who was a strong supporter of most minority movements, looked disapproving, whether at the absurdity of the names or the slight cast on the good respectable — even though in America almost obsolete — group of men known as grocers, it was impossible to say.

Both the Rushmores were curious about Annabel Lee, and Mary pushed on. 'I thought perhaps it was a stage name.'

'Oh no. My stage name is Irma Grese. Gene Beecham gave it to me.'

There was silence. Then Mary said, 'But wasn't she — '

'The Bitch of Belsen. Yes. I was the Bitch of Belsen.' She gave that wide-eyed look Dudley knew at them all, as she looked round the table to see how they took it.

Denny stopped laughing and adopted a thoughtful expression, the joker replaced by the sociologist. 'The interesting thing there is the tendency of events to turn into myth. What was Irma Grese like? We can't know because the popular image is Bitch of Belsen, that's the stereotype. And in time the stereotype replaces the real thing. Then even the stereotype changes. For another generation, those who're kids now, Bitch of Belsen will very likely be known as just the heroine of a horror movie — '

The Marstons never showed any hesitation about

34

interrupting each other, and Martha broke in.

'In a kind of way she was a feminist. I'm not defending her, but what she did was a kind of revenge for woman's experience of the male. Far too extreme, of course, but when you think —'

'Martha's got something there.' Denny nodded his head sagely.

'*Got something*,' Willie Rushmore said indignantly. 'What you've both got is poisonous rubbish.'

At the other end of the table, Dudley saw Annabel Lee was brimming over with repressed amusement. She provoked it, he thought. Now she said, with what he recognised as mock demureness, 'Lee says it's in bad taste.'

'Bad taste, that's the understatement of the year.' Willie scratched his bald head. 'But it's what you young people try for nowadays, isn't it, deliberate bad taste?'

Mary looked bewildered. She was a simple soul. 'But surely, my dear, nobody could think there was anything funny about Irma Grese.'

Her husband nodded, slow and solemn. 'Oh yes, *some* people do. *Some* people try to justify women like that.'

He glared at Martha. From that point on battle was joined, with moments of extreme acrimony being succeeded by passages of comparative calm. In one of these Mary asked whether Annabel Lee had used other names with different companies.

'Yes, but that was in England. This was my first job over here.'

'And you grabbed it,' Denny said. 'Let 'em call you what they like. The economic answer.'

'Oh, but it wasn't like that. I have a private income. I just do what seems to be fun, that's all. When it isn't fun I stop doing it.'

It was a very unsuccessful Christmas evening, and afterwards he told her so. She shrugged.

'Things seemed a bit dull. I thought it would be fun to stir them up.'

'Don't you think of anything but fun?'

'Not really.' She was sitting in the bedroom, in front of the dressing table. Idly she took the lipstick in front of her, drew a thick red line across her cheek, regarded it in the glass, then began carefully to wipe it away. 'Fun comes in fifty-seven varieties.'

Looking at her somehow disturbing action, he asked, 'Why me?'

'What d'you mean?'

'From what you've said you must dislike or despise almost everybody you've met at Graham. I'm like them. Different in some ways, of course, but we're all academic animals. So why me?'

'Because you're Lee and I'm Lee. And I fancied you from the moment I saw you.'

The answer was unsatisfactory, but it was the only answer he got. How could so many uncertainties, combined with so much that he did not care for, add up to happiness? Perhaps it is true, as some philosophical cynic has said, that we cannot know happiness without experiencing misery. Certainly his hours of pleasure in her company, hours in which on those fine November and December days they drove out in his old Dodge to neighbouring beauty spots, ate lunches in unpretentious little places with names like Joe's Shack, and then returned to the apartment in the fading light, drew much of their joy from his feeling that they were impermanent. Her pleasure in every new place and experience, the delight she showed when one day they were caught in a rainstorm and drenched to the skin, was something altogether new to him, and the occasional contradictions in what she said and did, the element of mystery involved in her very presence, were all part of the spell she wove round him. Although since, as he acknowledged, she showed no sign of doing these things with calculation, it could better be called a spell that he wove himself.

Three days after that unfortunate Christmas evening he sat in his carrel at the library marking students' essays when Willie Rushmore put his head round the door and asked if he could have a word. There was only one chair in the little study, and Willie perched uncomfortably on the desk. As often, he spoke in phrases that were not quite platitudes, yet sounded as if they came from last week's soap opera.

'I've talked with Mary. We agreed somebody must say it, and we like to think we're your good friends.' He shook his head mournfully. 'She's not right for you, Dud. You'll find it won't work out.'

'You mean she's too young? Nearly thirty, ten years' difference.'

'Not that. No, certainly not that. Just the sort of person you are, the sort of person she is.'

'You don't know what sort of person she is. How could you? I'm not sure I know myself.' He tried to explain something of what he felt, and to convey the unpredictable quality that attracted him so much. Willie listened without interruption, looking more and more like a hanging judge. At the end he shook his head again.

'You'll forgive an old friend's frankness. All that seems to me just drivel. You're a lonely man, always have been. This young woman has shown an interest, and it's bemused you. She's amusing herself, that's all, and she's chosen you as a subject. Nothing good will come of it.'

There was a lot more of the same, including reference to giving it to Dud straight from the shoulder. He listened patiently, for he was a patient man. Yet the words were meaningless to him, or rather had an effect opposite to what was intended, for they showed him the aching void that would be created if he lost Annabel Lee. Whatever she was like, no matter how much she alienated his friends, he knew that he could not bear to lose her. That night he asked her to marry him.

She rarely showed surprise, but did so now. '*Marry* you.'

'It isn't such an extraordinary idea, surely. We're living together, people are talking. I know you don't care about that, but I do. Besides —'

'Yes?'

'I can't bear to be without you. I want to be with you always.'

'People aren't together always.'

'What do you mean?'

'People fall in love and out of it. People die.'

'All right. Till death us do part.'

She shook her head. 'I'll spell it out just this once. I said I was a butterfly, or call it a free agent. I like that. I'm not getting married, to you or anybody else, do I make it clear?' The phrasing was harsh, but the laugh that followed enchanted him. 'Do you know, that hurt little boy look suits you?'

That night he dreamed she had gone. He called her by name, knowing that she was within earshot, but she did not reply. Running down corridors, expecting at each turn to find her, conscious of a thudding heart, he encountered the squat, grinning figure of Gene Beecham. *What are you doing here?* he asked, and Beecham said, *I have come back for her, come back to claim Annabel Lee.* Still grinning, he flapped his arms. *I am the cloud by night,* he said, *chilling and killing your Annabel Lee. My Annabel Lee, you understand, she is my Annabel Lee, the Bitch of Belsen is my Annabel Lee.*

He woke calling out, to find that he was clutching her body. The menace of the dream remained with him. They went on as they were, but from that night he felt that some destroyer would take her away from him. Yet there was no sign that this would happen. January was stormy, and there were no trips in the Dodge. Instead they played tennis on the indoor courts, and swam together in the outsize pool that was one of the prides of Graham. They went to drinks parties, including one at the President's house. Dexter greeted her with a professional twinkle, said that she was even more charming than he had heard, and complimented Dudley privately upon his Egeria, something that made him feel absurdly flattered. Her presence as his companion, that evening at the President's party, seemed — or so he persuaded himself — a guarantee that she would be with him at least until the spring. So, like many who have premonitions, he was dismayed when in February they were fulfilled.

The occasion was a reading of his works by a visiting English poet named George Garnish, whose book *Beasts* had caused a considerable stir on both sides of the Atlantic. The title was apt, for each poem celebrated a particular animal or bird, and all of them were notable for their savage attitude towards humans. No doubt it was natural for lions, tigers and panthers to tear strips of flesh from any human foolish enough to come near them, but in Garnish's poems dogs sprang at their owners' throats, cats scratched out children's eyes, household pets like white mice bit off the toes of babies. Garnish, a large genial man, read these accounts of horrors with much relish, lingering on the cracking bones, and on each scream of every victim. The hall was packed, an encore was called for, and the poet obliged with his *Ballad of the Hungry Pig*. Annabel Lee listened enthralled, and said so afterwards.

'Pure sensationalism. They sounded like Harry Graham's *Ruthless Rhymes*, except that those weren't meant to be taken seriously.'

'He was such *fun*. I'd love to meet him.'

The party for Garnish was at the Alumni House. They battled their way past the crowd at the drinks table to the place where the guest of honour, with several hangers-on in tow, was talking to the President. Dexter introduced them.

'I was telling Mr Garnish how much I admired the pure lyrical force of his poem about the escaped tiger. Such zest, such verve.'

'Such fun', Annabel Lee said. The poet's eye dwelt upon her momentarily. 'You sounded as if you meant it.'

'I did. But of course you're right, they're meant to be fun.' He said to Dudley, 'You're the seventeenth century man, aren't you? Those Royalist poets, Cowley and Cleveland and so on.'

'Yes.'

'Certainly carved out a place for yourself, nobody else reads them. Quite right too. Only Donne was any good of that lot.'

Dudley began to say that Donne was fifty years earlier than most of them, but before he could make this scholarly correction Garnish had turned away. Annabel Lee was with him, hanging on his words. Dudley suddenly felt depressed for no reason, got a large Martini, felt the lift of it hitting him and, again for no reason, thought about Elaine. Fragments of conversation moved around him, of a kind he had often heard, although that evening some of it was related to the poetry reading.

'— approach by definition ontological —'
'— is it clitoral, I said to Jake, or is it vaginal —'
'— affirmative action in the animal universe —'
'— here's the sum, blood plus bowels equals poetry, whadya say —'
'— poetry equals parody more like it —'
Halfway through another Martini he remembered that they had had drinks before leaving the apartment, because she had said she needed to be braced for the reading. It occurred to him that he might be a little drunk, a most unusual state of affairs. On the other side of the room he saw Garnish's big head bobbing, his hands waving eloquently. A momentary gap in the crowd revealed Annabel Lee among a knot of good-looking young men, all of them listening raptly to Garnish. He felt a pressure on his arm that in some way seemed familiar. Elinor was upon him, overwhelming in magenta, hair flowing freely below her broad shoulders.

'Wasn't that an experience? Something should be made of it, don't you think?'

He considered this with the care of the not quite sober. 'I thought Garnish made everything possible of those poems.'

'I mean something *dramatic*. Can you imagine the actual creatures on the stage, the words coming out through speakers all over the auditorium?' He shook his head to indicate no, he couldn't imagine it. 'Dud, this is Ira Wolfdale.'

A thin man emerged from behind Elaine. 'Glad to know you, Dud.'

'Ira's managing the Nickel Dollars. Have you seen them at the Drama Hall, they're just astonishing? I forgot, though, you don't like modern drama.' Elinor roared with laughter. 'Dud walked off the stage of an audience participation show a few weeks back, can you imagine? The Missing Link.'

'Don't know 'em.' Wolfdale had some resemblance to a wolf. He had a triangular head, hair cropped short, with long pointed ears and greenish-yellow eyes. A panatella was stuck in the corner of his mouth. 'Don't blame you, that audience participation stuff's mostly crap. The Nickel Dollar's a mime group, so at least you don't go deaf

40

listening to 'em.' When Wolfdale laughed the skin round his eyes crinkled, and he showed large pointed teeth. His extreme leanness made it hard to tell his age, which might have been anything between thirty-five and fifty. 'But Ellie's got it wrong, I'm not their manager, just doing a few chores because the man who runs 'em is sick. Along for the ride, you might say. Who's that across the room, the girl with Garnish?'

'Her name's Lee.'

'Annabel Lee,' Dudley said. 'Annabel Lee Fetherby.'

'She was with the Missing Link group, but she stayed on here.' Elaine added archly, 'She's a friend of Dud's.'

'Is that so?' Wolfdale took his panatella from his mouth, looked at it, stubbed it out in the ashtray. 'Good for you, Dud. Going to freshen this drink. See you later.'

The rest of the evening faded slowly in his mind. He found it difficult to escape from Elinor, who mentioned *that evening* as soon as they were alone. In the end he asked her to introduce him to the Nickel Dollars, whose silence was evidently confined to the stage. He remembered one of them, named Betty Lou, saying that she was just wild about the modern novel and didn't he agree Doctorow was really something, he recalled drinking two or perhaps four more Martinis and becoming involved in a discussion with some people in the English department about whether poetry should be approached intellectually or emotionally. At some point he looked round for Annabel Lee and couldn't see her. He had an uneasy feeling that he had asked Dexter where she was, in a rather peremptory manner. Then — but these memories grew dimmer and dimmer — he realised that she must be with Garnish, and searched for the poet without success. Perhaps he had another drink or two. And then he knew nothing more.

He woke thinking that he had been mugged. With eyes still closed he ran a hand over his head to find the bump that was causing such agonising pain. When he discovered nothing he cautiously opened his eyes. The pain increased, vari-coloured lights seemed to be stabbing his eyeballs. He groaned, turned over and slept.

When he woke again the pain in his head had been

reduced to a steady hammering, there were no coloured lights. He was in his own room, on his bed. His shoes had been removed, but otherwise he was fully dressed. The curtains were drawn, and he pulled them back to see daylight. His watch told him that the time was one in the afternoon. He had missed a class that morning.

The bed next to his was empty. It had not been slept in.

He saw this, but a censor in his mind refused to admit its meaning. He took off his clothes, groaning as each decisive movement of arm or leg brought an excruciating pain in his head. Then he turned on the shower, and stood under it for five minutes. After this he felt a little better, but the decrease of physical pain forced him to face the question: where was she? The answer was obvious. She had spent the night with Garnish. At the appearance of a celebrity, somebody younger and, he supposed, more attractive than himself, she had gone off without a word, without a thought.

He lay on the bed and wept.

It was several minutes later that an appalling thought occurred to him, and he went to the closet where she kept her few clothes. They had gone. So had her suitcase. He looked in the drawer where he had put her passport beside his own, one day when they had been talking — no, he had been talking, she took little part in it — about taking a trip to Europe that summer. The passport had gone.

He put his head in his hands and wept again.

A minute or two after that, he saw the note. It had been put on the mantelpiece beside the row of books he was using for classes, a bit of white paper torn from a larger sheet, quickly scribbled in her erratic handwriting. He read the few words several times, trying to find some subtlety of meaning in them:

Lee. End of the affair. Have to go. Sorry it's a rush. Love. Lee.

'Dudley, this is crazy. I can't allow you to do it.'

He said wearily to Willie Rushmore, 'No use talking, I've made up my mind. I shouldn't be away for more than twenty-four hours. You can cancel classes for the rest of the week, say I'm ill. If someone in my family had died, you'd do it.'

'But you are not ill, and nobody in your family has died. You're behaving foolishly, that's all. This might have happened at any time, and if you ask me you're well rid of her. If you find her, what makes you think she'll come back?'

'The note.' He took it from his pocket, put it on the desk between them. '*Have to go*. Don't you think she was trying to tell me something? *Sorry it's a rush*. Why was it a rush, how could there have been any rush? We were happy together, Willie. If she just wanted to say goodbye she would never have done it like this.'

It was just after four o'clock. They sat in the Dean's handsome panelled office. A framed picture of Mary stood on the desk, with another of their two children, and a third of the family group plus grandparents. Willie picked up the picture of Mary as if contact with it gave him strength.

'You're clutching at straws. You don't know that she's with Garnish.'

'Of course she is. You saw them yourself.'

He had been taken back to his apartment on the previous night by Willie and Mary, who had detached him from a furious argument with a professor of philosophy about the nature of reality. That was at about twelve-thirty, and they had seen the bulky form of George Garnish getting into a car outside Dudley's apartment. The car had then driven away. Willie and Mary, like the friends they were, had taken him in and removed his shoes. He resisted the further removal of clothing, so they had left him to sleep it off. Was the note on the mantelpiece? Willie didn't remember, and why should he do so? Now he said, 'I only saw Garnish.'

'She's with him. I saw the way she looked at him last night. You say his next reading is in Boston. She'll be there.'

'If she is, what can you do about it? No need to answer, I know you believe she was somehow forced to go.'

'There was a reason for her going, something that wasn't in the note. I must know what it is.'

'I notice you don't mention the first phrase, *End of the affair.*' Willie sighed. 'It all seems clear enough to me.'

He felt as if his head contained a spring so tightly wound that another turn would break it. He was relieved to hear himself speaking with the utmost calm. 'Willie, I can't argue. I'm going to find Annabel Lee and bring her back. I thought you would want to help me, but if you don't I shall go anyway.'

'All right. As you say, we won't argue. Today's Wednesday. I'll do the necessary covering up until the end of the week. If you aren't back by the weekend —'

'Of course I shall be back before then.'

Willie sighed again, and wished him luck. On the train ride in to Grand Central and the shuttle flight to Boston he tried without success to imagine what could have happened. He found himself overwhelmed by the sense of loss, and by the need to find her. He closed his eyes and saw not Annabel Lee but a butterfly, dazzlingly vivid, held and deliberately crushed by the alien hand. As it was crushed sparks flew from it, red, gold and blue, sparks so bright that it was painful to look at them. He opened his eyes, and the interior of the plane appeared to shudder momentarily. Was he running a temperature? He felt his forehead and found it cool.

At Logan he told the cab driver to take him to the Double Two Hotel, the address Garnish had given. The man was small and dark.

'You British?' He admitted it. 'You don't wanna stay there. Heard of the combat zone? Double Two's plum in the middle of it. You wanna find another hotel?'

'I've got a friend staying there.'

'You wanna change your friends. Okay, get in, your funeral.' He shifted a wad of gum from left to right in his mouth.

The cab was old and rocketed about. It was one of those with a window separating driver from passengers to discourage hold-ups, and a slot through which to push the fare. The card beside the meter gave the driver's name as S. J. Futrillo. He drove now, not fast but nerve-wrackingly, cutting in and out of the traffic, hooting occasionally. They went through the Callahan Tunnel into downtown Boston. Dudley's knowledge of the city did not extend much beyond Boston Common and Beacon Hill, and S. J. Futrillo took him into an unknown region. When he stopped the cab gave a final judder, like an exhausted horse. The payslot was opened.

'This is it.' He pushed the money through, added a tip. 'Thanks, mister. Watch yourself.'

He opened the door, stepped out. S. J. Futrillo drove away instantly, turned right with a screech of tyres. The Double Two had a narrow doorway, a neon sign outside. The whole street was bright with neon, flashing signs that said *Eaterie, Sexhibition, Pornocin.* Across the road, at the entrance to Pornocin, two blacks were distributing handbills to passers-by. Next door the neon said *Ten Girls Who Do It.* Mechanical sex, he thought, as he stood taking it in, the equivalent of the mechanical meals in McDonald's or Burger King.

'You like a little action?' A dapper black, tightly overcoated, hat at forty-five degrees, laid a hand on his arm. 'Boy or girl, any way you like, cost you fifty.' He shrugged off the hand, pushed open the door of the hotel.

The lobby was as narrow as the entrance. There was room only for an old sofa patterned with large red and blue flowers, and a counter behind which a young man sat reading the *National Enquirer.* He looked incuriously at Dudley. 'Rooms are ten dollars, pay in advance, twelve with shower.'

Years in America had not accustomed him to dealing with such denizens of a world to whom Graham was unknown, and arguments about the nature of reality as

45

incomprehensible as Greek. He was aware of uncertainty in his voice. 'Mr Garnish. He's staying here, I'm a friend of his. Can you tell me the number of his room?'

The desk clerk might have been anything between eighteen and twenty-five. His nose had been broken and badly reset, so that it was askew, giving him a sly look. 'Who says he's staying here? And who wants him?'

'I know he booked. I'm a friend. I want to surprise him.'

'Is that so?' He returned to the *National Enquirer*. The story was headed *Crazed Husband Slays Three*. After a moment he looked up. 'Still here?'

'Is Mr Garnish in the hotel?'

'Can't say unless I ring. Yeah, I know, you want to surprise him. Bringing him a present?'

'Not exactly.'

'Too bad.' He returned to the paper, and after a few moments Dudley understood. He took out a dollar and put it on the counter. Without looking up the desk clerk said, 'It needs friends.' Dudley replaced the single dollar bill with a five. The clerk pocketed it, looked at a dingy chart on the wall, said 'Four two four'.

On the way up in the elevator he felt an excitement he could not have defined. It was no more than a day since he had seen Annabel Lee, yet she seemed so remote that it might have been a year. He would see her, explain that her future lay with him and nobody else and that this parting had made him understand that, she would see this obvious truth and come back to Graham with him. His thoughts went no further as he knocked on the door.

A voice he recognised as Garnish's said: 'What is it?'

He had prepared a reply, one that could be called misleading yet was not positively untrue. 'It's about your lecture.'

The door was opened. Garnish stood there, bulky in vest and pants. 'The lecture's not till tomorrow, I don't know what the hell —' He stopped. 'Don't I know you?'

'We met at Graham. Dudley Potter.'

'Potter, of course. So what about the lecture, did they underpay me? Come in, have a drink.'

Garnish glanced behind him, then stood aside. The room

was large and old. Some plaster had crumbled from the ceiling, and the paint had peeled from the windows. There was a double bed with the cover pulled back and the sheets rumpled. A half-full bottle of Jack Daniels stood on a chest of drawers, with two glasses beside it. The sweetish smell of sex was in the air. A door led, no doubt, to a bath or shower. Was Annabel Lee in there?

'Plastic glasses, I'm afraid,' Garnish said as he poured the drink. 'All in keeping, though. I love the old Double Two, always come here. *Nostalgie de la boue* is what they'd say, I suppose, or some old cliché like that. They may even be right. Everything disposable, no holds barred, what more do you want as long as you can look after yourself, which I hope you can. And what *do* you want, by the way? Not a chat about seventeenth century prosody, I take it.'

He sipped the whisky, wondered why he was drinking it. 'Where is she?'

'What are you talking about?'

'Lee. She's with you.'

The big man stared at him, then shouted: 'Come out.'

The bathroom door opened, and a boy who could not have been more than seventeen came out, wearing only a pair of very short trunks. His body was extremely white. 'This is Charlie. Charlie, meet Dudley Potter.'

The boy's face was white as his body, white, tight and mean. 'Hey, what is this? Who's this guy?'

'I told you, Charlie. Dudley Potter.'

'I come up here with you. I don't know what you think you're into, but if it's a two on one with Mister *Dudley Potter* you can forget it.'

'It's all right, Charlie, I doubt if Dudley even knows what a two on one is. Here.' He passed over his glass to the boy, who drank while looking from one to the other of them.

'What's he want, then?'

'I'm trying to find out. You lie back and soak up that good drink.' The boy sat cross-legged on the bed, so that for a moment he was heartbreakingly reminiscent of Annabel Lee. Garnish said, still with perfect good humour, 'Who is it you're talking about?'

'Annabel Lee, she calls herself Lee. She was at the

reading, talked to you at the party. Afterwards somebody saw you getting into a car outside the apartment where she — where we live. This morning I found a note saying she'd gone. I'm trying to find her, and I thought she was with you. I'm sorry.'

'Think nothing of it.' The poet's big handsome face was thoughtful. 'Charlie, there's a tooth glass in there, will you get it.' The boy stared at him, did not move. Garnish lifted a shoulder as if to say *you see what they're like*, got the tooth glass himself, poured bourbon, drank. 'It's none of my business, and I don't approve of sticking my nose into things that aren't my business. However. For a man who knows all about seventeenth century poets nobody reads, you have to stretch a point. Yes, I remember your Lee. She liked what she called the ferocity of my poems, I said it was the animals that were ferocious, not the poetry. Then she drifted off. There were one or two likely lads I wanted to talk to.'

'But you saw her again.'

'That's right. She came up to me quite a bit later, said she'd heard I was leaving and had a car, could I take her to New York. I said no, I was driving to Boston. She said she had to get away at once, I don't know why. We ended up by me taking her to the apartment, where she picked up a suitcase, then to the bus station. She'd have got a bus a half hour or so later.'

'She left a note saying she *had* to go. Was she upset?'

Garnish went across to a closet, took out a silk dressing gown, put it on. 'Five minutes, Charlie,' he said to the boy who, with a furious look, got into bed and pulled the clothes over him. 'I wouldn't say upset, exactly. Disturbed but not upset, you might say, disturbed and excited. A girl who liked excitement, I'd say.'

And had been three months without excitement at Graham, he thought. 'Was she alone?'

'No.' Garnish saw that the answer was a shock, had perhaps been deliberately preparing the shock. In the poet's large rolling eye there was something amused, malicious. 'A man was with her, a lean and hungry Cassius-like figure. His name was Wolfdale.'

48

'Wolfdale?' he echoed incredulously.

'That's what I said. One of the things she had to get from the apartment was her passport, and in the car he asked if she'd remembered it. I don't know whether they went, but they were talking about going straight out to Kennedy and taking a standby flight to England.'

'Would you say she seemed to be willing to go with him?'

'Come on now, I was giving them a lift to the bus station, not a psychiatric examination. I told you she was excited, and I suppose you might say he looked pleased with himself. Make what you like of it. And now Dudley, my old seventeenth century friend, I'm saying goodbye. Some pleasures improve with keeping, but not if you keep them too long.'

'I'm sorry.'

'All right. Whatever you're looking for, I hope you find it. And look out, it's a great big hungry world out there. Don't let it eat you up.'

The poet's hand was laid on his shoulder in a friendly gesture. Then he was outside the door. Downstairs the desk clerk was still reading his paper. The hungry world outside did not eat him up. He got safely back to Graham.

'Frankly, Dud, you look awful,' Willie said. 'Not so much as if you'd seen a ghost, more as if you are one. You've got to forget about her. Isn't that so, Mary?'

'She was just no good,' Mary said. She was as kind-hearted as Willie, and had at her disposal as large a collection of clichés. 'No good at all.'

They sat in the Rushmores' living room after lunch, with a log fire burning in the grate. A gentle snow, the first of the winter, was falling, and it had become bitterly cold. The changed weather seemed to symbolise his severance from Annabel Lee, as though the Graham in which she had passed those months no longer existed. It was Saturday afternoon, he had been back on campus for more than thirty-six hours, and there was no word from her. Why should he have expected any word after her note, Willie asked? But he had. The pale face and despairing eyes he had seen in the glass that morning had indeed something ghostly about them. He knew the need for action, and what the action must be. That was what they were talking about.

'You're not thinking straight.' Willie had got his pipe going, and now puffed out smoke in a way that seemed to Dudley in his present mood to exude self-satisfaction, although in the past that same pipe-smoking routine had seemed a guarantee of stability in an erratic world. 'It's an obsession.'

The tight spring in his head twanged, and he lost control.

'For God's sake what do you know about it?' Then he said, 'I'm sorry.'

'That's all right, Dud.' Mary was prepared to be understanding. 'Sticks and stones may break my bones, but words will never hurt me, as my mother used to say.'

Willie took it up. 'This man Wolfdale. Would you suppose he was an old flame?'

'I've talked to Elinor. She says he's some kind of theatrical producer, has a lot to do with little theatre companies. He told me he was standing in for the manager of the mime company up here, and apparently that was true. So it looks as though they must have met by accident.'

'Let's consider what it is you're proposing. We're less than half-way through the semester. You're going to give up your classes and go to England on a wild goose chase. What good can come from it? None that I can see. When will you be back, a week, a month, six months? You don't know, so it means cancelling all your classes for the rest of the semester. It isn't responsible behaviour, Dud.'

'Are you saying it can't be done?'

'I'm saying it's a piece of foolishness. I can do it, yes. I can tell Dexter, and anybody else who's interested, that you're under great mental stress, which would be true. There'll be some inconvenience for your students, and some of them will moan and groan, but that isn't the problem. What you should think about is that although Dexter is a tolerant man, none more so, he won't like it. This isn't like a request for a sabbatical, it's just taking time because you feel like it, and saying to hell with the curriculum. That's the way people will see it, and you can't blame them.'

He heard the words, yet they carried no meaning for him.

They belonged to the existence in which Professor Dudley E. Potter tried to show students why the author of *The Raven* and *Annabel Lee* was a good but not a great poet. Did it matter what the students thought, since they would be going out into a world in which poetry was of no importance to them? The image of Annabel Lee came into his mind suddenly, laughing, saying *Never Mark Antony dallied so wantonly* . . . He put a hand to his head.

'Dudley. Are you all right?'

'Yes yes.' He groped back desperately to something Willie had said. 'An obsession, that's right, perfectly right. I have to go to England, Willie, I must find out.'

The smoke curled up from the pipe. 'How will you go about it?'

'I have a friend. someone who knows her, acts for her legally.'

'What if there's nothing to find out?'

He could have wept, screamed, throttled the complacent figures who turned their concerned faces to him. Instead he said there was no use in talking, and left. Outside the snow was falling more thinly now, and he walked home through it. He approached the Hospitality Residences with a quickening heart, in hope that he would see the light telling him that she had returned. She would have an explanation, he would accept it, ask no questions, everything would go on as before.

When he turned the corner there was no light in the window. The rooms, empty of her presence, brought tears to his eyes. There was no towel on the bathroom floor, no cigarette stubs, the place had its old, and now unbearable, neatness.

It took half an hour to get through to England. Then he heard a woman's voice.

'Phyl?'

'This is Phyllis Shilton. Who is that?'

'Phyl, it's Dudley. Dudley Potter.'

A pause. 'Why, *Dud*, this is just *fantastic*. Where are you?'

'At Graham. Phyl, I have to come over to England, and I wanted to talk to Steve —'

'But Dud darling, it's wonderful. Hang on a sec.' He could

hear her saying that it was Dud, Dudley Potter, coming over, then she was back on the line. 'Dud, it's been a life-time, we can't *wait* to see you. I'll put Steve on in a sec, but of course you must stay here, there's oceans of room.'

'That's very kind, Phyl, but I'd thought of a hotel.'

'Nonsense, I won't hear of it. I'm putting Steve on now, but mind, it's settled, you come straight here.'

It was years since he had heard Steve's voice, and it was somehow a relief to find it sounded just the same, deep and rich, much more impressive than his own measured and even in youth slightly professorial tone.

'Is that true what Phyl said, Dudley, that you're crossing the water? When'll it be?'

'As soon as I can get on a plane. Tomorrow if I'm lucky.'

'The sooner the better, and you'll stay with us. Phyl will be mortally offended otherwise, and you wouldn't want to cause her a mortal wound, would you? What's all this about? Are you coming to a conference on seventeenth century poetry? World-wide of course, with a strong South American contingent?'

'I want to talk to you about Annabel Lee.'

'Who?'

'Annabel Lee Fetherby. I think your firm handles her affairs.'

'Featherby?' A pause. 'What in the world is she to do with you?'

'I'll explain when I see you. But that's right, isn't it, you do handle her affairs?'

He felt relief when Steve agreed that they were her solicitors. There was no reason why he should think that she had been telling lies, yet to have this confirmation seemed somehow a proof that their relationship still existed.

He felt unable to face another session with Willie and Mary, and instead wrote a letter saying that he had to go to England, and asking Willie to make any explanation he could. The whole of his life at Graham seemed to belong to a world with which he no longer had any connection. As the plane rose from Kennedy on Sunday night, and New York's lights gleamed below him briefly like a child's sparklers, he felt that he was moving towards some inevitable destiny.

PART TWO

1 *A Room in World's End*

When he left England the Shiltons were recently married. Steve had just been taken into the family firm, and was complaining about the boredom of it, Phyl was an aspiring actress, in and, more often, out of work. They had just bought a flat in Kentish Town, and were busy furnishing it. Of course he had known that it was no longer a flat but a house, and that they had graduated from shabby Kentish Town to smart St John's Wood, but the house they lived in and the way they lived came as a surprise.

The house was a detached early Victorian villa in one of the roads near St John's Wood High Street. A six-foot wall concealed the neat front garden. The door was opened by a girl who said she would call Mrs Shilton, and took him through a large hall into a drawing room furnished in green and gold. The furniture was in varying shades of green, the walls were covered by gold wallpaper with a green design, a corner cupboard held what looked like valuable bits of porcelain, some of the landscapes on the walls had their own small lights to illuminate them. Windows at the back showed what must in summer be an elegant garden. His feet sank into thick gold carpet. There were no such rooms in Graham.

The door opened and there was Phyllis, arms wide. He just had time to observe that she had put on weight before being folded in her embrace.

'Dud, *wonderful*.' The warmth of lips on cheek, nostrils touched by some delicate scent, then he was being held at arm's length. 'You look just the same. No you don't, you're thinner, and that's an interesting pallor or perhaps it's just the journey, was the plane too awful? Steve's at the office, longing to see you this evening, but if you want to have a word he's at the other end of the line. Adrian's at boarding school, but you'll see Rosemary later on, she's a trial but also a poppet, even though her mother says so.' She dropped his arms, struck herself on the forehead. 'What am I thinking of? Are you famished? Or jet-lagged, flaked out, want to collapse on a bed? Darling, you must *say*.'

Phyl's style had always been enthusiastic, but had she gone on like this always? Had he just forgotten? He saw his room, which was in blues and greys, had its adjoining bathroom, and made his apartment at Graham look like a slum. The girl brought in coffee and little cakes, and while eating them he tried without great success to focus on what Phyl was saying. Perhaps he was jet-lagged after all? He missed the tail-end of a sentence, and found that she was regarding him with amusement. Broad-faced and with a peasant coarseness about her features, she might have been called plain but for her liveliness and her wide enthusiastic smile.

'You're saying nothing, darling, that means no entanglements. I can't believe it.'

'Entanglements?'

'*No* little affairs, it seems unbelievable, you're holding out on me. I used to think you were the most attractive man I knew after Steve. And you weren't so backward. Remember that evening at the Cromwells? In the swing?' He remembered nothing about the swing, had even forgotten the Cromwells. Was he to be confronted by another *that* *evening*? 'Of course that was before Elaine. Do you hear from her?'

That he was able to answer. 'No, I've heard nothing from Elaine since I left.' He waved a hand embracing the gold and green, the porcelain and the pictures. 'All this. Foolish of me, I suppose. I wasn't prepared for it.'

She gave her throaty chuckle. 'Avoiding any mention of the swing. You never did *say* much, Dud, I remember, though you *looked* volumes, but darling, did you expect to find us still in that poky little flat? Steve's the senior partner now, you know, although his heart's really in Otter Books, the publishing operation. Everything's splendid, we have the most lovely life, two beautiful children, *except* —'

'Except?'

'Except that one's not twenty-five any more. And that Steve's always busy. But I don't know what I'm saying or why, when I just started out to tell you it's so good to see

you again, darling Dud. And look now, here's Rosemary.
Say hello to our old friend Dudley Potter, Rosemary.'
'Hello.' Rosemary was eleven or twelve, with features like
her mother's but more delicate. 'Dudley Potter, that's a silly
name. If I had a name like that I'd change it.'
'That might have been a good idea, but it's too late now.'
'Mummy says an old friend. You don't look so very old.'
'Thank you.'
'I'll tell you something else. You don't talk like an
American, not the way you should. The last American who
came here called the garden the back yard.'
'She's supposed to have a tummy upset, but I think she
stayed away from school just to see you,' Phyl said. 'That's
enough, Rosemary. If you're well enough to make nasty
remarks you're well enough to go to school.'
'I'm not.' She waved a hand. 'See you around. That's
what they say in America.'
'You're looking very *worn*, darling,' Phyl said after
Rosemary's exit. 'Are you sure you wouldn't like to lie down
for a couple of hours?'
He said no, but in the next moment felt his eyes closing.
He undressed, lay down in the blue and grey bedroom,
closed his eyes and immediately evoked a picture of
Annabel Lee as he had last seen her, at the party for
Garnish, with a gilt choker round her throat. He had bought
the choker, a gift she had only permitted because it was
cheap. It had come from the Al Jewelry Store in
Graham — jewelry, he thought, an American spelling
perversion like sox and eaterie, and then no no, it's an
established old-fashioned alternative to jewellery, indeed
wasn't jewellery the commercial term and jewelry the
veritable spelling, oh Annabel Lee what was it you wanted
more than jewelry, I am lost without you . . .
When he woke the curtains had been drawn. He looked
at his watch and saw that he had slept for eight hours. The
thought of Annabel Lee stayed with him while he took a
bath and dressed. As he went down the elegant staircase
he heard a male voice, and when he entered the drawing
room Steve came across and hugged him.
Steve had changed less than his wife. In his mid-twenties

he had been big and awkward, with the curved nose, high colour and aggresive jollity of Mr Punch. Now he had filled out, the hair was slipping back from his forehead. He was recognisably the same jovial Steve, however, and the student aggressiveness had turned into authority. It was no surprise that he was senior partner in his law firm, and a successful publisher.

Steve was one of the few people who had never abbreviated Dudley's name, and he had not changed in this respect either. 'Dudley, you don't look a day older, younger if anything. That's what life in the academic cloister does for you. Now, the first thing is a drink. Then we can put our feet up and ask each other what happened to old so and so, and you can tell me what connection you've got with the erratic Miss Fetherby. Remember her, love? She came to dinner once a few years back.'

'Do I remember? She was asked because she's a client of Steve's, and he said she was interesting.'

'So she is,' Steve called over from the drinks table.

'Is that what you call it? We invited Aubrey Painton, Judith Clark and a couple of other actors *all* for her benefit, and what does she do? Hardly eats a mouthful, barely speaks to Aubrey who sat next to her and couldn't have tried harder, says she thinks the only interesting work now is done by little theatre companies, and the commercial theatre is finished. You couldn't get more *West End* actors than Aubrey and Judith, it was a real insult. Then she left at ten o'clock, never wrote to say thank you. I mean, honestly, Dud, don't you think that's a bit much?'

He was about to say that he recognised the kind of behaviour, and that an imp of perversity seemed to get into her at times, when Steve held up a hand. 'Later, later. Dudley told me on the phone that he's here in connection with Lee Fetherby, so he can tell us the story after dinner. Or tell me, if it's man's talk.'

'Not particularly.'

'Glad to hear it, otherwise Phyl would never have rested till I told her about it afterwards. Now, let me give you a run down on what we're doing at Otter.'

Then, and through most of the excellent dinner cooked by

Phyllis, but served by the living-in maid he had seen already, Steve talked enthusiastically about the new fiction, drama, poetry and educational books being put out by the firm he had taken over a couple of years back when it was semi-moribund. Phyl listened with the rapt absent expression of one who had heard it all before. Rosemary punctuated the narrative with sighs of boredom before going off to watch television. She fired a parting shot just before leaving.

'Geraldine's father says you're over-extended, Daddy. That doesn't sound very nice.'

'I agree, my love. Who's Geraldine's father? And who's Geraldine, come to that?'

'She's a girl at school. And her father —'

'His name's Harkness,' Phyl said. 'He's some sort of banker.'

'City and Country Capital Trust, I know them.' Steve wagged a finger at his daughter. 'I've got news for Geraldine. Tell her you hear rumours around the clubs that *her* father's so much over-extended he's liable to burst. All right, Phyl, no need to look like that. Better say nothing, Rosemary, treat her with the contempt she deserves.'

Afterwards Dudley asked whether these publishing activities didn't affect Shilton, Mallett. 'No problem, my boy. I've got good workhorses and an omniscient new secretary. I've learned the art of delegation.'

Later they sat in a room that, as Steve said in a tone that nicely blended apology and pride, they called the library because it did contain a lot of books. There was a fire in the grate, brandy was poured from a decanter, Steve lit a fat cigar, and Dudley told his story. The contrast between this affluent life and his frugal existence at Graham was powerfully present to him even while he was talking. In such surroundings the tale he told had a flavour of absurdity, and his emotional problems seemed not so much unreal as unimportant.

Such a feeling was not, however, reflected in the reactions of either Steve or Phyl. Steve let the cigar go out, and when he had finished Phyl came over and embraced him.

'My poor darling Dud, what you've been through. But what a bitch.' He began to protest. 'Sweetie, surely you must *see*. She just likes making trouble, the way she did that evening here at dinner, and she picked you because — oh, because you're you. Darling, it's truly romantic of you to come haring across the ocean, but you must see it won't be any good.'

'Dudley hasn't come all this way for comments like that, Phyl. He'll have had plenty of those back at Graham. What I don't see is what you think you're going to do. I'll tell you what I know about Lee Fetherby, though I don't know how much it will help.' He relighted the cigar.

'First of all, what she said about the family background was true. My father was old Brigadier Scudamore's solicitor, so we dealt with the estate when he died. The way it's come through to Lee, which is what she calls herself, is as she said. The interest provides her with a reasonable income, and the capital goes to her when she's thirty, which if I remember is in about three months' time. I'd have to look up the exact date.'

'How much is the capital?'

'It'll probably amount to something over a hundred thousand. After all deductions, though that's only a rough estimate.'

'Supposing she died before she's thirty?'

'You have a powerful imagination, Dudley. Not much room for it to operate here, though. Her mother took up spiritualism in her last few months, and if Lee should die before coming into the inheritance it goes to the World Spiritualist Council or whatever it's called.'

'Nothing for the other sister, Lenore?'

'Nothing for Lenore. I never met the lady, but I gather Rose Fetherby didn't approve of her way of life. I did see Rose two or three times. She was a rum old bird, I can tell you. Thought she was a spiritual descendant of Edgar Allan Poe or some such nonsense.'

'And her brother-in-law, Stewart Fetherby? Did he make a lot of money?'

'I believe that's so, but I've had no dealings with him. I don't see that he could tell you anything.' For a moment Mr

Punch looked aggressive. 'Let me fill you in a bit about Lee. I didn't meet her at Rose's funeral — I was busy, and my assistant Paul Race stood in for me — but later on she asked my advice about things connected with the estate. She used to ring up with queries, and come into the office occasionally. She was an oddball, and oddballs interest me, always have. I took her out to lunch a couple of times, and as you've heard we asked her to that rather disastrous dinner. I think that was almost the last time I saw her. She moves around quite a bit, no need to have a job, so it isn't easy to keep track of her.'

'You did, though. You knew she was at Graham.'

'Is that so?' Steve looked surprised.

'I found one day that she was getting mail at the Post Office. She said it was her money from England. That was in January.'

'I didn't know that. It must have been arranged by my secretary, Jean Cousins. Paul would know about it, may have fixed it himself. He's my indispensable man at the office, I shovel all sorts of donkey work onto him. Anyway, she'd naturally have been in touch to make sure she got her allowance.'

'What was she like?' A ridiculous question perhaps, yet he was aware of having seen Annabel Lee only in one place and one context. Perhaps in another she might have seemed a different person.

Mr Punch looked thoughtful. 'Attractive, but there's no need to tell you that. Absolutely independent, wayward — wacky, call it, and that's a good word. Never settled anywhere, had a flat around the Oval, though I believe she gave that up a few months ago, Jean could tell you. She just got in touch when she wanted something, very self-absorbed, very sold on the offbeat theatre groups she messed around with. Not much help, I'm afraid. Why don't you look in at the office? Jean or Paul Race might be able to tell you something more, though I doubt it.'

'She never talked about her friends?' Steve shook his head. 'And you've never heard of Wolfdale?'

'No. Shall I tell you what I think? I'm going to anyway, you know that.' Mr Punch grinned. 'Skip all the stuff about whether it was sensible to come over or not, assume you know what you're doing which seems to me by no means certain. Say you're right about the note she left, which you produce as if you were giving us a glimpse of the Crown Jewels, and that she was somehow forced into going away. Assume all that and what in the world, my dear old Dudley, do you think you're going to do about it?'

'Find Wolfdale. Talk to him. And find her, take her back with me.'

'And if she repeats "End of the affair", which is what she's said already, what then?'

He found it hard to reply. 'If she says that — really says it to me, with nobody else there —' He put his head in his hands. 'I don't know.'

'Steve,' Phyl said reproachfully. 'Dud came to us for help, not to be cross-examined.'

'Perfectly right. Dudley, me boy, take no notice of a hard-bitten old lawyer, on with the quest for Wolfdale. You say he's some sort of theatre producer. Now, who do we know in production? Phyl, can you think of anyone from your glamorous past?'

'You may think it's a silly suggestion, my darlings, but have you tried the telephone directory?'

And indeed, there they found *Ira Wolfdale Promotions*. The address was 28 Rasputin Street, SW10. There was also an I. Wolfdale at 34 Malcolm Court, Putney. When they rang there was no reply from either number. Before the evening ended they had planned his strategy for the following day. In the morning he would call on Wolfdale Promotions, and if he got no satisfaction would try the Putney flat. In the afternoon he would call at Steve's office, in the hope of finding out more about Annabel Lee. As they talked he felt concern and friendliness seeping from Steve and Phyl, a warmth that almost embarrassed him.

When Dudley was a student at King's College he had shared a flat with Steve, Elaine and another girl named Maggie something or other, in the area off the King's Road known as World's End. The flat was cramped, the façade of the late Victorian house visibly crumbling. A chunk of brick-work fell down one day, narrowly missing Steve. Dudley had half-expected to see that part of Melitter Street demolished and replaced by blocks of flats, but the houses stood there still, hardly recognisable behind their refurbished brickwork and fresh facings. Flowers in pots grew in the once neglected front gardens, the front doors were newly painted. The houses were now occupied, he supposed, by the young executives whom he had read about when he saw English papers, couples who ran wine bars, public relations men with wives who did something or other in television. Turn a corner, though, and in another street there was the World's End he had known, a builder's yard, a car park on a bit of waste land, houses with dirty and boarded-up windows and broken front railings. With the advancing process of decay had come an increase of violence in the slogans chalked on walls. ARSENAL RULE OK, they said, ALL BLACKS AND YIDS OUT, KILL A PAKI TODAY, BIG BREASTED BITCHES ARE BEST. Two boys in their early teens were chalking the wall beside the car park. As he came up they ran off giggling. Below a crudely-drawn pitchfork he read STICK IT UP.

Rasputin was one of the unreconstructed streets. There were holes in the road surface and great cracks in the pavement, as though a subterranean force was pushing its way up, and about to burst out of darkness into day. Fifteen years ago the street had perhaps been decently shabby, now the rotting houses looked fit for the bulldozer. Twenty-eight was no better or worse than many. Curtains were close drawn in the front room. He pressed the door bell but heard nothing, then pushed the door. It opened, and he found himself in a narrow hall, with posters on the walls advertising theatre companies, among them *Revolutionary Impulse* and *Tory Scum*. A murmur of voices came from a room on the left, and he turned the door handle.

There were three people in the curtained room. A girl sat at a desk, with a telephone and a typewriter in front of her, a man leaned against the mantelpiece and another sat in a chair facing the girl. The man standing up was big and wide, built like a blockhouse, with close-cropped reddish hair. The man sitting down was bearded, young and thin, with discoloured teeth. The girl was spotty, sported long earrings, and was chewing gum. They all wore jeans and pullovers. There were more posters round the walls. A couple of filing cabinets gathered dust in a corner.

The three stared at him. The girl said, 'What do you want?'

'My name is Potter. I wanted to see Mr Wolfdale.'

'You can't. He's not here.'

'Can you tell me where I might find him?'

She shook her head and continued to chew. The bearded man asked: 'What you want him for?'

'It's —' On the spur of the moment he said, 'I represent a theatre group. I was told Mr Wolfdale might be able to help me.'

'Is that right? What name?'

'The company, you mean?' Imagination gave him wings. 'The Flying Aztecs. They zoom round the stage on wires. It symbolises nuclear attack on our cities.'

'Never heard of 'em. You, Fanny?' The girl, whose verbal stock seemed exhausted, shook her head again.

Dudley said to the blockhouse, 'What about you? You belong to a theatre group, I suppose. What is it, Revolutionary Impulse or Tory Scum?'

The big man stared at him, apparently baffled. 'Leave it off.' He spoke to beard. 'I'll be away then.'

'Right, Ginger.'

'If there's anything —' A nod of the big head might have been directed at Dudley. 'Give me a bell.'

When the front door closed beard tilted his chair back, lit a cigarette. 'Now, what is it? You don't belong to no bleeding theatre group. What you after?'

'I told you, I want to see Wolfdale. This is his business, isn't it?'

'Right, but we kind of run it, see? Haven't seen Ira since, when was it, Fanny, Friday?' Fanny nodded.

'That was after he got back from the States. Was he on his own?'

The legs of the chair bumped down. 'If you know about that trip —'

'Dingo,' the girl said in a neutral voice. Dingo stopped

talking. A look passed between them which Dudley could not interpret, then Dingo spoke again.

'Fanny, you got something to do.' She nodded and went out. Dingo said, in a tone markedly pacific, 'Look, chum. We're just here to make bookings for groups, okay? Ira's got his private affairs, not our business, and he don't like it if we poke our noses in. I'll tell you the best I can do. You leave a number, tell me where he can find you. I'll see he gets it as soon as he's in touch. If he wants to talk he'll give you a bell. How's that?'

'I suppose it will have to do. Does the name Lee Fetherby mean anything to you?'

'Not a thing.' Certainly Dingo showed no reaction to the name.

'When do you expect to hear from him?' He could hear the girl talking in another room, but the words were indistinguishable.

'Could be in ten minutes, could be tomorrow. He's in touch most days. What's the number?'

He knew the address, but he could not recall Steve's number. They found it in the book. With that he left.

He walked up the New King's Road. Opposite him a winking sign said Pizza House, and in the course of a hundred yards as he walked towards Sloane Square he passed a McDonald's, a Kentucky Pancake House and a restaurant called The Great American Cowboy, which had a gigantic ten gallon hat modelled in plaster above the entrance. A supermarket window showed apples so perfectly coloured that they looked like wax or plastic, bearing a ticket: *French Golden Delicious*. The feeling that he was in an Americanised England, a country that had lost its identity, added to the sense of unreality that had been with him since he emerged from the womb of the plane at Heathrow. The boys writing dirt on walls, French Golden Delicious, Pizza Houses and McDonald's, had not existed when he was here fifteen years ago.

A mirror in the window of a shop called Jetset Clothes showed him a figure neat, bewildered, strangely innocent. The home of that figure was surely not here but in Graham. What ridiculous compulsion had brought him here, did he really believe that Annabel Lee was in danger, or was his quest as hopeless as that for the Holy Grail? No doubt sensible Willie and friendly Steve were right, but they had no answer to the quickening of his pulse when he thought of her. He said to the figure in Jetset's mirror: 'Next stop Malcom Court Putney. First of all, a sandwich.'

Rejecting the Americanised food places he went into a pub called the Dove and Eagle. This too was not a pub of the kind he remembered. Great plastic birds brooded over the bars, eagles with long curved beaks and plumage that looked like rusty iron, doves almost as menacing in their milky whiteness and pink-eyed stare. The motif was repeated at the back of the cubicles round the room and even on ashtrays, eagle and dove blending in what might have been peaceful accord or devouring enmity. He ordered a pint of beer and a sandwich, but found no free table. The boys wore black leather jackets and studded belts, with shirts that had the Union Jack across the front with NF in the centre. The girl had spiky hair dyed dead black, and tight tartan trousers. When he asked if the seat was free they nodded, and went on talking.

'Watcher doin' tonight then, Andy?'

'Dunno. Might go down to Brixton. 'Eard there might be some fun.'

'I was told Kensington,' the girl said. 'They're boarding up some of the shops in the High Street.'

'*Kensington?* Get out.'

'What abaht Notting Hill? Do a couple of Paki shops.'

'No good, the pigs are lookin' out there. They got it wrapped up, Notting Hill.'

'I 'ate the Pakis,' one of the boys said. He stuck out his feet so that one of his heavy boots jarred against Dudley's shin. Dudley moved his leg away. 'They smell. That food they eat, they stink of it. And they got no bottle.'

'Leave off,' the girl said, looking at Dudley. He finished his beer, conscious of their eyes on him. A sign in one corner of the room said "Gents". As he opened the door he saw that they were still looking at him.

He had finished at the urinal when he heard the door open. He turned. The ginger-haired blockhouse stood in the doorway grinning. He was fitting brass knuckles to his right hand. In all the years at Graham, Dudley had seen violence only once, when State troopers charged to disperse students during the troubles at the end of the sixties. Now he put his hands joined together in a gesture of appeal. The blockhouse advanced on him, big fists raised, muttering the cliché phrases preceding physical attack: 'Sticking your nose in — teach you a lesson —'

He felt but hardly saw a blow in the stomach that made him gasp, brought tears to his eyes. A second blow meant for his nose caught him on the side of the face instead, and flattened him against the wall. The blockhouse, still grinning, blew on the brass knuckles. From some self-help manual looked at long ago, Dudley remembered an illustration showing a bully attacking a woman who, as he lunged towards her, kicked him on the shins. Mind communicated to leg, he lashed out with his right foot, and made contact. The blockhouse grunted with pain and retreated a couple of steps. Dudley took another flying kick, but this time found air. A blow in the ribs made him gasp. Another on the chest and he collapsed to his knees. He felt his collar grasped, he was pulled upwards, the blockhouse murmured happily, '*Now.*'

The door opened. One of the black-jacketed boys came in.

'What's up, then? What's he done?' He laid a hand on the blockhouse's arm.

'Keep your two pennyworth out of it. This is private.'

'Not now it ain't. Let go of 'im.' A knife appeared in his hand, long and thin. The blockhouse relinquished his grip of Dudley, and looked at the boy in astonishment.

'What's up with you? He's just a bleedin' busybody I'm teaching a lesson. What you want to give me aggravation for?'

''Cause the NF's for Queen and Country, that's why. On your bike now, I got friends upstairs.' Grumbling inarticulately, Ginger retired. The boy helped the shaken Dudley up, and brushed off his coat and trousers, talking all the time. 'Thought you was a long time down the pisser, mate, you don't want to get the wrong idea about us, we got nothing against whites, just these bleedin' coloureds we'd like sent back where they belong, the way old Enoch says. How you feelin' then?'

'Not too bad. Thank you very much.'

'You a stranger here?'

'I was born in England, but I live in America.'

'And you got the right idea. No bleedin' freedom here, I can tell you, can't do what you want without the pigs after you all the time. No work either, though work's a bleedin' drag. Right then, mate, I'm off.'

And he was gone. Dudley straightened his tie, and saw that apart from a bulging cheek he looked undamaged. His ribs felt a little sore, but otherwise he seemed unhurt. There was no sign of the leather jackets in the bar, and he regretted not being able to buy them a drink, until he felt for his wallet and found nothing there. That, then, had been the reason for the solicitous brushing down. The wallet had contained more than twenty pounds, but fortunately he had another five in his hip pocket. It had also held Annabel Lee's parting note, for whatever use that might have been. He realised now that when Dingo had sent Fanny out of the office it must have been to call the blockhouse and tell him that the unwelcome visitor should be followed and roughed up.

But why should innocent and reasonable enquiries cause him to be roughed up? He felt indignant, and the incident increased his determination to find Wolfdale, whether at Malcolm Court or elsewhere.

2 *Background of a Dead Man*

Malcolm Court was a block of flats like a hundred others in London, five storeys high, looking out in front on the busy Upper Richmond Road, at the side on a street leading down to the Thames. Like all its kind the block had an air both slick and impermanent, as if it had been made quickly from children's blocks and might very soon be dismantled and rebuilt in a different form. Even the entrance hall smelled new. There was no liftman or commissionaire, but a notice told him that flats 30 to 39 were on the third floor.

When he rang the bell of 34 it opened almost instantly. A man in a shiny blue suit stood in the doorway and said: 'Who are you?'

'I'd like to talk to Mr Wolfdale.'

'Or you wouldn't be ringing his bell. What's your name?'

He was about to say that it was none of the man's business, when a voice called: 'Let him in, Jackson.'

The man in the shiny blue suit stood aside. They were in a hall so tiny that they almost touched. Three doors led off it, one of them half-open, and the man who had spoken appeared in this doorway. He was very tall and thin, with dark hair parted in the middle, and a mouth which turned down at the corners.

'You wanted to talk to Wolfdale. Come in.' They entered a large living room with a picture window. In Upper Richmond Road lorries thundered by. 'There he is. You can say what you like, he won't talk back.'

And there he was, recognisably Wolfdale, and evidently dead. He had been shot once, through the side of the head, and lay on his back looking up at the ceiling. A little blood had seeped onto the mushroom-coloured carpet. A revolver lay on the carpet just beyond the dead man's outstretched right hand.

'My name's Bleek, Superintendent CID. What's yours?'

'Potter.' It was years since he had seen a dead person,

and he could not stop staring at the body.

'Making you uncomfortable? No accounting for tastes. Let's leave him, and come and tell me about yourself. We've finished with him, and I was just on my way. Been sorry to have missed you.' The turned-down mouth moved upwards briefly. This was evidently a joke. Bleek led the way into a bedroom which contained a double bed, a fitted wardrobe and a chest of drawers. On the walls were prints of a Spanish dancer and the Grand Canal, of the kind found by the hundred in not very good hotels. The bedroom, like the living room, might have been occupied by an anonymous person, Mr Nobody. Bleek sat on the bed and made a gesture towards a chair. 'Friend of yours, was he?'

'No. I'd only met him once. In America.'

'But you came calling on him here. You must have had a reason, Mr Potter. Sit down and tell me what it is.'

He told the Superintendent the truth, not because he was under any illusion about honesty being the best policy, but because he could think of no other remotely adequate story to tell. He said that Miss Fetherby and he had lived together, and that he believed Wolfdale had somehow compelled her to come to England with him. He ended with the visit to Rasputin Street and the incident at the Dove and Eagle, not even omitting the theft of his wallet. Bleek listened with frowning concentration, but the wallet story prompted again the rictus that served him for a smile.

'An innocent abroad,' he commented. 'Or an innocent come back home. You'll see a few changes. We can't match New York or Los Angeles for crime yet, but we're moving up, top of the second division you might say.' The idea seemed to make him positively cheerful. 'So that's your story. Takes a bit of believing.'

'You mean you don't believe it.'

'Didn't say that. Just that your lady friend may be into something more complicated than you realise. Or she realises.'

'You've found no trace of her?'

'Can't say we've been looking, since we didn't know she existed. She's not living here, if that's what you mean. Look at the place. Bedroom, bathroom, no sign a woman's stayed the night. Wolfdale used it when he was in London, kind of transit camp for him, that's all. May have brought a bird here sometimes, but strictly a one-night stand.'

'You speak as though you knew him.'

'We did, Mr Potter, we did. Mind emptying your pockets? And then take off your trousers.' It was a demand, not a question, and Dudley obeyed it. He emptied the contents of his pockets on to the bed, handed over his jacket and trousers, submitted to a brief but thorough search. 'Okay, get dressed. Sorry about that, but I had to make sure.'

'Make sure of what?'

'Make sure I wasn't being conned when I called you an innocent abroad.'

The door opened. Jackson said, 'They're taking him away now, Chief, all right?' Bleek nodded, and the door closed again.

'I told you we knew Wolfdale. He was an agent. Do you follow me?' Dudley shook his head. 'Used these fringe theatre companies for moving drugs from one country to another. Hash, heroin, coke, speed, you name it. Never carried it himself, wasn't a handler, just fixed for one of these actors, if that's what you call 'em, to handle the stuff. Not that I've got anything against fringe companies, saw some good shows up at the Edinburgh Festival a few years back. Subversive, mind you, against Queen and country, but good. Wolfdale never got anything but rubbish.'

'So when I called at Rasputin Street, the people I saw —'

'They knew what Wolfdale was up to, right. Probably thought you were a reporter from one of the nationals doing a drugs story. In disguise, you might say.' The rictus appeared. 'Thought they'd teach you a lesson.'

'Since you know about Wolfdale, why wasn't he under arrest?'

'Hard to explain to an amachoor like yourself. We put him away for a stretch a few years ago, and he didn't like it. Ever since, he's co-operated. Given us details of who was taking what where, so we could keep tabs on it.'

'You made arrests through his information?'

'Sometimes. If we made too many we'd have blown him, he'd have been for the high jump. More useful to us the

71

way he was. Keeping tabs on the stuff, that's what's important.'

'You mean you knew about the movement of drugs, and just let it go on.'

Bleek sighed heavily. 'I said I couldn't explain to an amachoor. Mr Potter, we can monitor the movement of drugs, we can control it when things get hot and heavy, but we can't stop it, not while there are sellers and buyers. Drugs is big business, it's international, and no laws I know are going to make the trade go away. Why am I using my valuable time filling you in on all this? Because somebody stopped Ira's mouth, and I'd like to know why. He was killed yesterday afternoon, the doctor says. Cleaning woman came in and found him this morning.'

'The revolver was in his hand. I thought he'd killed himself.'

'Then you thought wrong. I knew Ira, he was good company as long as you bore in mind you couldn't trust him further than you could throw him. He wasn't a suicide, never would have done it. That's not just my opinion either. He was shot through the right temple, the shooter was by his right hand, but he was left-handed. I ought to know, he always had matches but never ciggies, so he'd cadge one and then strike the match on the heel of his left shoe. Add that there was no mark of burning round the wound, so the shot wasn't fired close to the temple, and you've got a clumsy attempt to make a killing look like suicide. Now, the boys he dealt with might have knocked him off if they found he'd been crossing them. Or they might not, many of them being as reasonable as you or me. But if they did say good-bye to Ira, they'd have made sure it was known, kind of a lesson to other people. Or that's the way I read it, though I could be wrong. If I'm right, though, it makes me wonder.'

'About what?'

'You may have noticed, since you're a wordsmith trained for a bit of subtlety, that I didn't answer when you asked if I'd found any trace of your Miss Fetherby, just said we hadn't been looking for her. Well, we did find a trace, if you call it that. There's a little second bedroom with a desk in it, and among a lot of stuff about the theatre groups, and some letters from birds, of whom Ira pulled quite a few in his time, we found this.'

It was a marriage certificate, giving details of the marriage of Ira Jacob Wolfdale, of Malcolm Court, Putney, and Annabel Lee Fetherby, spinster, of 18 Rapping Lane, Kennington. The date was eight years ago.

'I can't believe it. Why didn't she tell me?'

'Oh come on, Mr Potter,' Bleek said with evident enjoyment. 'Innocence is one thing, but that's downright silly. Would she tell you something like that?'

'I don't know, perhaps not. She didn't talk much about herself. But her husband turning up like that out of the blue — I remember he looked across the room and asked who that was, as though it was somebody he hadn't seen for a long time — that might explain why she went away with him.'

'Not really.' Bleek was still enjoying himself. 'Because in the same bunch of letters and documents were some from a firm of lawyers about their divorce, which took place eighteen months after the marriage. So if he had any hold on your young lady, it wasn't to do with their marriage.'

Shilton, Mallett's offices were in New Square, which with its large centrepiece of green grass, gleaming Bentleys, Rovers and Volvos parked side by side, some with waiting chauffeurs, and legal dogsbodies walking from one block to another with extreme decorum, gave the impression of having slowed down the pace of life like a slow-motion camera. This, Dudley supposed, was a little like his remembrance of English life, yet since he had left in the early days of the Beatles, the swinging sixties as people were calling them now, no doubt his recollections were almost completely wrong.

That vision of a peaceful past vanished when he entered the offices, which were full of indirect lighting and black and chromium furniture, with abstract paintings on the walls instead of the traditional cartoons by "Spy" of Victorian legal lights. Steve sat behind an oval table done in black-and-white stripes, in a big swivelling chair that had the same zebra markings. Above him was the biggest metal lampshade Dudley had ever seen. The bulbs within its semi-circular curve cast a fierce white light onto the desk. Steve, cigar in the corner of his mouth, was talking on the telephone. A young man sat at the other side of the desk going through a bundle of papers.

'Cannot be done,' Steve said in his most aggressive Mr Punch voice. 'Sorry, no can do. Can't be did. *C'est impossible*, as the Frogs say, *comprenez*? Miss Otis regrets, Mr Shilton apologises, but he's not interested. I *have* considered everything, my friend, and that's the verdict. And goodbye to *you*.'

He put down the telephone, beaming. Dudley saw that his shirt matched the chair and table. 'Nothing to do with soliciting, don't get the wrong impression. Somebody wanting us to pay over the odds at Otter for one more book about Hitler, all about how the war affected his sex life. I

74

wouldn't have bought it anyway. How do you like these offices? Never seen anything like them, I'll bet. The idea is to get right away from the leather chair and dusty file legal image. My word, Dudley, what's been happening to you?'

He realised that Steve was referring to the marks on his face. 'I was mugged and then robbed.' He explained, without mentioning his visit to Malcolm Court, which he thought might be kept for Steve's ears alone.

Steve shook his head in disgust. 'I don't know what London's coming to. Still, glad you're here in one piece. My God, I'm forgetting my manners. This is my right-hand man, and left-hand man too, Paul Race. My old and dear friend Dudley Potter, Paul.'

He had gathered the impression, from Steve's words on the previous night, that Paul Race was a grey-haired old reliable, not a bright young man with a ready smile.

'I know your name already, Mr Potter. Steve has often talked about you.'

'That's right. If you'd been a fly on the wall, Dudley, you'd have blushed to hear me invoking your name when Shilton, Mallett have been engaged in something particularly time-wasting or mucky. You're my shining example, I say to Paul, the paragon I might have been, living a worthy life engaged in useful research and teaching the young what to read and how. There are times when I envy you, Dudley, you don't know how much.'

His face, which was made for liveliness and laughter, settled into an expression of gloom. It had always been hard to know whether Steve was joking or serious. Dudley said, 'I'm flattered, but you know that's all nonsense. You were always a man of action.'

'True, my boy, perfectly true. Yet sometimes — well, you see how I bore young Paul here with chat about you and the past. You can put away that stuff about the Rawnsley Trust, Paul. Deal with it yourself, it's too fiddling for me. It's the grand design that's always interested me, not the details.' The young man closed the folder. 'What we need now is everything available about Miss Annabel Lee Fetherby.'

'Formerly Mrs Wolfdale,' Dudley said when Race had gone out. He told Steve about Wolfdale's death, and

75

Annabel Lee's marriage and divorce.

'Beaten, up, robbed, and then a dead body. You may not have a lot of money, but you quiet academics do see life when you get going.'

'Did you know she'd been married?'

'I didn't. No reason why she should have told me, but it may be somewhere in the papers.'

And sure enough, when Race returned with the thick file there, almost at the bottom, labelled *Fetherby* with *Scudamore Estates* in brackets below it, was a note about Annabel Lee's marriage and divorce, and the resumption of her maiden name. The file also contained a copy of *Cooking Through the Year.* Dudley leafed through it, and was touched that she had made for him two or three dishes mentioned in the little book — a proof, he thought, that those who write the recipes are often less good at the practical job of preparing them. The details of the estate were as she had said, and she had full use of the capital sum at the end of June, in a little over four months' time.

'As you may have gathered, Paul, Dudley is a friend of Miss Fetherby. She's disappeared, and he's trying to find out where she might be now. I told him she's got a flat in Kennington.'

'She had. She gave it up some time late last year. Here we are, it was at the end of October. She wrote to us on her very ancient typewriter.'

The letter was erratically typed, on a machine with a ribbon whose inking was faulty, so that the type had faded here and there. It read:

Dear Steve,

I have decided to give up this flat, as I shall be travelling around for the next few months. I may go back into fringe theatre, there are several possibilities. Anyway, I think I've had London for the present. Will you sell what remains of the lease for me? I'll keep in touch.

The letter was signed *Lee Fetherby.*

'You must have seen this. It begins "Dear Steve".'

Steve grinned at him. 'Naturally it does, my boy. I told

you I'd taken her to lunch, and she'd been to dinner. And I recognise that typewriter, I've seen several letters written on it. It was like her not to get a new ribbon. No doubt I saw the letter, but I wouldn't have dealt with it. Paul did that.'

Race laughed. 'Not exactly. It was a routine matter. She had a short-term lease, I think for only three years, which had been renewed. We'd have sold the remainder of it, no doubt. Jean handled the details.'

Dudley was looking at the letter. 'Another thing. The address on this is 14 Rudderley Gardens. When she got married her address was somewhere else in Kennington called Rapping Lane.'

'Can't help you there, nothing about any other address in the papers. Very likely she lived there before she came into the income from the inheritance. Ah, here's Jean.'

Jean Cousins, Dudley saw when she came in, was the real doer of donkey work. Steve's secretary was a woman in her late fifties. She had iron grey hair, a pair of spectacles worn on a chain round her neck, and was inclined to bridle at any suggestion that her behaviour in any business matter might have been other than impeccable. She bridled a little now as she said that they had been able to settle the matter of the lease quite amicably with the owners. There had been a small financial adjustment which would be found in the accounts.

'Did you visit the flat at all yourself?' Dudley asked.

'Indeed I did.' Dudley's identity had been explained, but the mere putting of a question was enough to place Mrs Cousins on her mettle. 'I went round to make sure everything was in order, and to collect the keys. Which were delivered to the owners' agents on the following day.'

'Was Miss Fetherby there?'

'She was not. The place was empty. No furniture, nothing at all. Which surprised me. Seeing that Miss Fetherby is a quite unbusinesslike person — I suppose you might say she has the artistic temperament — I expected that some clearing-up might be necessary, and was prepared to give instructions accordingly. Happily, there was no need to do so.'

Paul Race said, 'She sent us a letter from America, and I passed it on to you.'

Jean Cousins inclined her head graciously. 'That is so, Mr Race. It was to say that she wished to have her quarterly remittance sent to an address she gave. That was done accordingly. I hope there is nothing wrong.' The clear implication was that if any mistake had been made, she was not the person responsible.

'Nothing at all, just checking details,' Race said with a smile. 'I've got the letter here. And I'm right in thinking that we have heard nothing from her more recently? This is our last communication?'

'That is correct,' Jean Cousins said, with a tinge of scorn at the idea that the question should be necessary. She retired, and Race passed across the letter. It was in what looked like Annabel Lee's hand, although Dudley had seen little of her writing, and it simply asked that her quarterly payment for January should be sent to the Post Office at Graham.

'Did either of you go to the Kennington flat?' Steve, who was burrowing in the file, shook his head.

'I never went there, no reason to,' Race said. 'Why do you ask?'

'I was wondering if she had friends in the place, someone she might have talked to. The way she left seems to me rather strange.'

Steve looked up. 'She was a strange lady, as you should know.'

'Her ex-husband has been killed — '

'Probably all to do with drugs, as that policeman said.'

'I don't understand,' Paul Race said. 'What's that about her husband?'

Dudley explained about his visit to Malcolm Court. 'So you see, it's not just a matter of my being foolish, in case you thought that, Mr Race. I shall go down to Kennington. And I thought I'd go up to see her uncle in Yorkshire. Do you have his address?'

'What in the name of God do you want to talk to him for?' Steve asked. 'He can't have seen her for years. Oh, all right, all right, I came across it just now in this file. Here it is. Brattick House, Naborough, Yorkshire.'

Race coughed. 'If I may say so, something like this has happened before, when she decided to travel. That is, we had no address from her. But she always gets in touch in time to make a request for her allowance.'

'But that won't be until April. I should like to know where she is now.'

'Mrs Waddington,' Steve said, waving a piece of paper extracted from the file. 'She's the cleaning woman at the house Rose Fetherby was living in when she died. You may as well have her address too. Though I'd like to put it on record that trekking up to Yorkshire to see some retired supermarket owner is the wildest wild goose chase I ever heard of. And now, my boy, Phyl is impatiently expecting us, and I propose to take you home before some Dickensian villain garrots you in New Square.'

4 *The Flat in Kennington*

The changes in a London that during his fifteen years'
absence seemed to have been covered by a glossy
pseudo-American glitter which in places ˙had peeled away to
reveal the diseased wood beneath, were not immediately
apparent at Kennington Oval. The gasometer loomed over
the cricket ground, the approach by way of Harleyford Road
still had its proper British dinginess of uninviting pubs and
hopeless-looking cafês with hand-written menus in the
windows offering eggs, bacon, sausages and mash, with tea
the way mother makes it, for what seemed remarkably little
money. Here he had come with his father, handsome
Doctor Potter, to watch England play Australia or the West
Indies. 'Ignore the surroundings, my boy,' his father had
said, when he exclaimed at the ugliness of the gasometer
and the mean little houses at the back of the ground. 'Or
relish them rather, the contrast between the dreary shapes
of industrial London and the gallant knights of sport jousting
upon the greensward.' Who but his father would have used
such a word as "greensward"? At thirteen Dudley, a conventional boy, had been uneasily aware of Doctor Potter's
habitual loud voice, and his theatrical gestures.

There was no sign of a greensward, or any green thing, in
Rudderley Gardens, which was a row of small Victorian
houses in a state of decay much less advanced than
Rasputin Road. Cars lined both sides of the street, packed
so closely that it was hard for one used to the American
habit of leaving a reasonable distance between vehicles to
see how they could be disentangled. There were net
curtains in some windows, a woman was even to be seen
washing the steps outside one house. No doubt Rudderley
Gardens would have reached the Rasputin Road stage in a
few years, but it would go down fighting.

The door of number 14 was open, and outside it a woman
stood talking to the milkman. She was a big woman in her

80

fifties, she wore an apron, and her hair was in curlers.

'Doesn't live here any more,' she said in response to his question. 'She moved out a few months ago, isn't that right, Johnny?' The milkman nodded. 'What was it you wanted, then?'

'I'm a friend of hers.' He gave what he hoped was a winning smile. 'I wonder if you could spare a few minutes to talk about her. Just to answer one or two questions.'

'Talk about her, I could do that. But I wasn't expecting company.' A simper lightened her bulldog features. 'You'll have to give me a minute or two, I can't talk looking like this. All right, then. Just a pint today, Johnny.'

The milkman produced the pint. It occurred to Dudley to ask him where he would find Rapping Lane.

'Rapping Lane, mate? Where will you find it? Answer is, you won't. Knocked down a few years back when they put up the Harold Wilson Council Estate. Remember Rapping Lane, Mrs M?'

'I certainly do. That lady you're asking about, she had a room there once, she told me, just for a few months.'

'She knows everything,' the milkman said admiringly. 'If Mrs M can't tell you what goes on round here nobody can.'

'That Johnny, he's rather familiar. My name's Mrs Morris,' the woman said as she showed him into a spotlessly clean front room crowded with furniture. 'And you're Mr —'

'Potter. Dudley Potter.'

'Pleased to meet you, Mr Potter, though I can't say I remember her mentioning the name. But then it was always a job to get anything out of her. You just sit down, and I'll be with you in a jiffy.'

The jiffy proved to be several minutes, during which he sat in an uncomfortable armchair which was part of a three-piece suite in uncut moquette. When Mrs Morris returned she had taken out the curlers, removed the apron, and sprinkled herself liberally with eau-de-cologne. She carried a tray on which stood a teapot, two cups and some biscuits.

'There we are,' she said when she had poured two cups, and he had refused a biscuit. 'A cup of tea mid-morning is very refreshing, I always say. You'll forgive me mentioning it, but that's a nasty bruise on your face.' He said that he had run into a door last night in a strange house and she nodded, apparently satisfied. 'So you're a friend of Lee's. She was always what I call close-mouthed about her friends, was Lee. Keep yourself to yourself if you like, I said to my Ronald, and Josie Morris is the last to want to know somebody else's business, but she carried it too far. Not but what she was always perfectly pleasant, mind you, nothing to complain of at all. Artistic, of course.'

'I notice you call her Lee.'

'That was her name, wasn't it, Lee Fetherby?'

'Her full name was Annabel Lee.'

'I don't know about that, she was always Lee to me. When I found out what her name was, that is. She had the first floor, we're on the ground, so naturally I saw quite a bit of her, but it was always Miss Fetherby this and Mrs Morris that, and you can't go on that way, can you? So I said to her one day, quite directly because I believe in speaking straight out, my name's Josie and my husband is Ron, and what shall we call you? So then she laughed and said, my name's Lee. The first two or three years — she was here around five years altogether — she had jobs off and on. I remember her working as a waitress. I said to her, why do a job like that with your education, why don't you get something better? Because you could see she'd been properly educated, if you understand what I mean, her voice and that.

'It satisfies me, she said, gives me enough to live on, though really what she wanted was to get on the stage.' Mrs Morris leaned forward, and almost upset her teacup. 'Mind you, it wasn't the stage as I understand it, not a nice West End play nor even the National Theatre, that wasn't what she was after. It was all these — I don't know what they call it, put on plays in pubs and such —'

'Fringe theatre.'

'That's it. Well, this fringe theatre, often you get paid peanuts, or even nothing at all. She's a nice girl but she's got a screw loose, Ron used to say. Then her mother died and she came into money, or got a big allowance, and of course she had no more need to work, though mind you she still sometimes did that fringe business. There were times when she'd be away for, oh, six or seven weeks at a time. Then when I'd ask what she'd been doing — oh, not straight out, I'd say I hoped she'd had a pleasant time or something — she'd just say yes, thank you, very enjoyable. I mean, you'd think she'd have mentioned where she'd been.'

On the contrary, he found it only too easy to imagine her resisting Mrs Morris's good-natured curiosity. He asked if she had many visitors.

'Quite a few, but never, you know, anyone really regular. Mostly those fringe actors I expect, funny-looking people. Used to be some queer smells coming from up there, she was a great cook, I believe she'd even written a book about it. But I'm not sure all the smells were cooking.'

'How do you mean? I don't understand you.'

'My Ron — he's in insurance, you know, sees a lot of the world — said he wouldn't be surprised if they were drugging. Though I wouldn't like you to think I was suggesting that, just they were such funny-looking people, often you couldn't tell the men from the women. Mind you I never really spoke to any of them, just saw them on the stairs.'

'I see.'

'Nothing like that about Mr and Mrs Consett, who're up there now. Mr Consett works for the Council, Town Hall job, you could set your watch by when he goes out and comes home. Mind you, I got to be fond of Lee. Ron, he didn't see her that often, and didn't altogether take to her, but I liked her even if she was what you might call standoffish. She had a way with her, specially when she wanted something and gave you a look out of those big blue eyes. Ron and I, we were never blessed with children, and I came to think of her quite as if she was my daughter.' Mrs Morris produced a handkerchief and dabbed her eyes, so that a strong wave of scent was wafted towards Dudley. At the same time she seemed to become aware that she was conducting a monologue rather than responding to questions. On a faintly suspicious note she said, 'How was it you never come here, if you're a friend of hers?'

'I didn't know her at that time. We met in America.'

'Reelly.' To Mrs Morris, it was clear, America was a land

of fable. 'Are you perhaps in the theatre yourself, if you'll excuse my asking?'

'No. I teach in a college, and Annabel Lee came up there with a fringe group.'

'*Reelly.*'

'And we became very friendly.'

'Do I scent a romance?' Mrs Morris asked archly. 'Ron and I would be ever so pleased. And perhaps it would explain things.'

'What things?'

'Why, the way she left. Going off like that. I was really hurt, I can tell you. I've got my feelings like anybody else.'

A limited measure of candour seemed likely to hold appeal for Mrs Morris. 'I don't think I had anything to do with her leaving here, because we hadn't met then. But we did become very friendly, and she stayed on at Graham, which is where I teach. Then she just disappeared, went off, as you say. I know she's returned to England, and I'm trying to find her. She left here suddenly?'

'Suddenly, I should say so. I'll tell you just what happened, but I must have another cupper to help me along. Will you indulge, Mr Potter?' When he had said no, and she had poured her second cup, she went on.

'Near the end of October it was, and she'd been away a few days, nothing unusual in that. Then one Thursday — I'm always out on a Thursday, it's bingo afternoon, and Ron gets home before me — when I got back Ron says "Miss Screw Loose has been back" — I told you that was what he called her sometimes, only in fun of course, "And gone again". So I said how's that, and it seems he heard the front door open, thought it was me, and called out. She called back, "It's only Lee", and he went out in the hall and saw her. She told him she was just packing up a few things and then she'd be gone again. And then not much more than a quarter of an hour later she called out "Just going now, goodbye". That was the last he saw of her, and the last I saw too. What a way to leave a place, not even saying goodbye to your neighbours. A few days afterwards, some-one came round from the solicitors who look after her affairs, said she was giving up the place for good. I never heard anything like it.' The handkerchief was used again.

'What about her furniture? It was disposed of, wasn't it?'

'I'll tell you about that. *That* was a queer do, if you like. The next week, Tuesday I think it was, there's a knock at the door, and outside is Crundall. "Come to clear out the first floor", he says. And I says, not so fast —'

'Who is Crundall?'

'He calls his place a furniture shop, but it's mostly junk. And he does light removals as well. Not so fast, I said, what's your authority? I felt sure there must be some mistake, because this was before the lady came round from the solicitors. You could have knocked me down with a feather duster when he takes out a bit of paper. It's written and signed by her, and it asks him to clear out the contents of the flat as she's got no further use for them. She hopes what he sells them for will more than defray the cost of collection.'

'You say it was handwritten. Are you sure it was her writing?'

'Well, yes, I think so. I mean, it looked like her writing, but I only read it the once. You don't think there was something fishy about it?'

'I think it shows that for some reason she wanted to get away from here quickly, just as later on she wanted to get away from Graham quickly. Did she ever mention a man named Wolfdale, or did you see him? A tall thin man, with hair cut very short.'

'I don't remember anyone like that.' She returned to her story. 'Not so fast, young Crundall, I says. There'll be private papers up there, all sorts of personal stuff I daresay, and it's my belief this is some sort of practical joke. So I went up with him, he unlocked the door — she'd sent the key with the letter — and would you believe it, she'd cleared out all her personal stuff. Toilet things, papers, letters, clothes, everything. Must have done it that very day she saw Ron.'

'You say papers and letters, but you don't know that there were any. Or nothing private. Do you?' Mrs Morris reluctantly admitted that she didn't. 'She has very few clothes, or at least that was so in America. Everything went into a single suitcase.'

'I don't know about that, but I can tell you, Mr Potter, I cried. I came down here and had a really good cry. To go off like that, I call it heartless.'

Perhaps she has no heart, he thought but did not say. 'There must have been some compelling reason. So Crundall took away the furniture?'

'Yes. It wasn't worth much. It's true there were only bits and pieces, nothing like this.' She fingered lovingly the arm-chair she sat in.

The shop facia said, in lettering scrawled as if by a child, *Crundall's Junktique.* Inside there was a variety of objects few would be likely to buy. He noticed chipped and broken statuary, a brass hunting horn, a lacquer table lacking one leg, an enormous dining table, a piano with some keys missing. The man who came out from the back was small as a jockey, and had a bowler hat on the back of his head. He acknowledged his identity with a knowing smile, as though he had avoided some kind of trap.

'Jack Crundall it is. What can I do for you, squire?' When Dudley asked if he remembered collecting the furniture from Rudderley Gardens, the smile became more knowing. 'I hope you're not going to say there's money owing on that stuff, because believe you me that isn't so, there wasn't anything worth a light. Here, lemme show you something.' He accompanied Crundall to a small room at the back, chiefly occupied by stuffed birds and animals inside glass cases. Shifting an otter and a mouldy-looking spaniel, Crundall lifted from the floor a typewriter with six rows of keys instead of the usual four. 'This came out of that flat, must be sixty years old or more.'

'Does it work?'

'After a fashion, but who's going to buy it? Museum, you say, but it ain't happened yet.' He peered at Dudley. 'My word, squire, you ran into a heavy door, didn't you? Or should I ask you how the other feller looks?' He laughed heartily. 'Anyway, that's the sort of stuff it was, real rubbish. It was Jack Crundall's good nature and her being a nice girl, that's why I took the stuff.'

'There's no question of any claim. You knew Miss

Fetherby, did you?'

'Not to say *knew* her. She used to come down for a drink at my local, the Goat and Compasses, and I chatted her up a bit.' He tipped the bowler forwards, gave Dudley a wink. 'Didn't get to first base, though. She was a loner. Or maybe, what do they call it, a lezzie.'

'Did you see her with other people?'

'A few times, didn't much like the look of them. Didn't pay much attention after I'd made my play and she'd said no dice. Little but good, that's Jack Crundall, he doesn't have to beg for it. Then when I got that note —'

'Do you still have it?'

' 'Fraid not, squire, this was four months ago or more. When I got it I came over all excited, it's not every week you get a letter saying come and clean out my place and keep the cash. And then, even though it began "Dear Sir" I recognised the name from meeting her in the pub. Lee, everybody called her there. But when I saw what was there —' He shrugged, and pushed the bowler back again.

'You didn't find anything personal among the things she'd left?'

'Certainly didn't. If there had been, the old battleaxe down below would have been on to it. She was standing over me the whole time. What's your interest, squire, may I ask?'

'I believe she may be in trouble of some sort. I'm trying to find her.'

'If you do, blow her a kiss from Jack Crundall.'

5 *The Golden Ball*

Phyllis had given him a key to their house. The contrast between its luxurious calm and the shabby gentility of Rudderley Gardens was marked. Which of these worlds represented reality, which was a proper home for Annabel Lee? The house was silent and empty as he went up the gently curving staircase into the blue and grey bedroom, and tried to make sense of what he had learned in the past forty-eight hours. The hurried departure from Kennington and the move across the Atlantic suggested that Annabel Lee had been running away from something, but what? It was a shock to him to learn that she had been married to Wolfdale, yet what possible threat could a divorced husband have posed? Had Wolfdale been killed because of his connections with drugs, or was his death something to do with her? He believed still that she had been forced to leave America and was somehow in danger, but with these thoughts went awareness of an element of absurdity in his quest. *End of the affair* — the words were decisive enough. What would he say if Annabel Lee came in at this moment and asked —

A gentle knock sounded on the door.

He scrambled off the bed, called a welcome. Rosemary's head appeared. He was conscious of disappointment, and said inanely: 'I didn't know there was anybody here.'

'Only me. Mummy's out. Daddy's at the office. That is, at his publishing office. He left a message to tell you that. In case you wanted him.'

'Thank you.'

'I bet you didn't hear me.'

'No, I didn't.'

'I like it when people don't know I'm there. I should like to be invisible. Then I should know what everybody said and did, I should have power over the whole world.' Invisible, he thought, invisible Annabel Lee. She came further into the

88

room. 'I heard daddy and mummy talking about you. Daddy said you were looking for the impossible.'

'Did he?'

'He said your trouble was you'd always been searching for an ideal woman, and real ones could never live up to the ideal.'

'I don't think he'd like you to pass on everything he says.'

She considered this. 'All right. There's a message for you. From Mr Race at the office — not the publishing office, the other one. He asked you to call him.'

When he got through to Race the young man sounded politely excited. 'We've got a lead on Miss Fetherby that may be worth following up. I was looking through the correspondence again and found a letter sent in June last year from an address in Fulham. In it she says she's staying a day or two with a friend. I rang the number and spoke to the girl, the friend. Her name's Tess Barlow and she's apparently some sort of an actress, not a very good one I should guess. She's in a show at the Golden Ball, that's a pub in Islington. She'll be there tonight, and said she'd talk to you then if you went along.'

'Do you think she knows where Annabel Lee might be?'

'She wouldn't say much to me, but I understood she'd seen Miss Fetherby recently.'

'How recently? Do you mean this week?'

'I think so, yes. But she was either a bit fuddled or being cagey. Anyway, there it is, if it's any help.'

'It's very good of you. Thanks very much.'

'Happy to be of use. Are you still planning to go up to Yorkshire tomorrow?'

'Unless I learn something from this girl that changes my plan, yes.'

'Why not have lunch with me first? I'll have done a bit more digging into the papers by then, and may have come up with something else. Steve only gave them a quick onceover — his heart's in publishing at present, and as you probably know he doesn't like detailed work.'

They fixed a lunch date, and Dudley hung up. He looked at his face in the bathroom mirror, and admired the fading blue-brown bruise round the cheekbone. Apart from that he felt only slight soreness from the blockhouse's punches, and reflected that he must be in reasonable condition.

Later on he told Steve and Phyl about Race's call, over a drink in the drawing room.

'Paul's very good,' Steve said. 'Not the greatest legal brain in the business, neither am I for that matter, but he's marvellous at checking details.'

'And dishy, distinctly dishy. Can't *think* why he's not been snapped up.' About Phyl this evening there was a kind of languorous contentment, the air of a cat gorged on cream. 'I think your shiner is just adorable, darling Dud, it quite positively *adds* something.'

Steve contemplated the solid gold balls in his shirt cuff, and pursued his own line of thought. 'Paul's taken a lot of weight off me at Shilton, Mallett, so that I can concentrate on Otter, but in some ways he's as crazy as you. Do you know what he's threatening to do? Shake England's soil off his feet. And for what, I ask you? To run a farm out in Brazil.'

'*Brazil*,' Phyl said with a gasp. 'He *must* be crazy.'

Dudley was momentarily diverted from his own concerns. 'Does he know anything about farming?'

'It's in the blood,' Steve said gloomily, as if farming were a disease. 'His father and grandfather were farmers, but at least it was here, not in Brazil. If he's serious, and I still don't know if he is, he must have a Brazilian girl friend or something like that. Mind you, I can understand him being bored by the legal life, I find it pretty tedious myself. You made the best choice, Dudley, no doubt about it. I want you to promise something. If this woman, whatever her name is, really has seen the Fetherby girl in the last couple of days, I want you to give up looking for her.'

'Why?'

'Because, for God's sake, don't you see it will mean she was telling you the exact truth in that note, saying that your affair was over. Finished. Kaput. That's the only thing that makes sense, as you'd see if you weren't living in a fairy tale.'

'I'm searching for an ideal woman, not a real one?'

'Exactly.' Steve showed no awareness that his own words

were being quoted back to him.

'Would you say that had been my trouble with Elaine?'

Steve looked into his glass, and did not reply. Phyl leaned forward.

'Darling Dud, what we're saying is we love you dearly, and we think Miss Fetherby's a little tramp, and we hate to see you agonising about her. You're so *romantic*, Dud.'

'Is that my trouble then, being romantic?' The sweetness and friendship he felt flowing from them both disturbed him. 'The things you're telling me I've said to myself, but whatever my trouble is I've got to go on, do you understand? I have to *know*.'

'She has to tell you herself?'

'I suppose so. And something else. Elaine lives up in Yorkshire. If I go up there I shall talk to her, if she's prepared to see me.'

They both stared at him, then Steve burst out laughing. 'Dudley my boy, there's no need for other people to give you a hard time, you do it to yourself, and I can only hope you enjoy it.'

That wasn't always true, he wanted to protest. In the long years at Graham he had been content to annotate John Cleveland, to correct the failings of erratic scholars. Elaine had been pushed firmly into the furthest corner of the most distant cupboard at the back of his mind, Annabel Lee had not existed.

'I hereby renounce my role as spiritual adviser.' Steve got up and slapped him on the shoulder.

'Steve, you are *ponderous* at times.' The look husband and wife exchanged might almost have been one of dislike on her side, reproach on his. 'Are you going to say what we had in mind, or shall I?'

'We're not going to let you get away without giving you a party,' Steve said. 'It's no good asking what your plans are because you don't have any, but you've got to be here on Saturday night, is that firmly understood? People have already been asked, even though it's at short notice. No will not be an acceptable answer.'

The Golden Ball was in a side street off City Road, near the

Angel, and Dudley arrived in time to catch most of the play, although he wished afterwards that he had spent the time in the bar.

The piece was called *The Name of the Game*. It took place in an upper room of the pub, without the benefit of scenery or stage props. The audience sat in chairs grouped in a rough semi-circle, and the actors made their exits and entrances through the door that led down to the bars. The play was about two women who were constantly being brutalised by their men. Both men were out of work, one was a revolutionary and the other a reactionary, and there was a good deal of talk about the pressures of society on the individual. The women were similarly divided, but the reactionary woman lived with the revolutionary man, and the revolutionary woman with the reactionary man. It seemed to Dudley that the beating up might have been avoided by a simple change of partners, but when this actually took place the result was that the two revolutionaries killed the two reactionaries. At the end the survivors held up the hatchet and the knife with which they had disposed of their partners. 'The name of the game is violence,' she said. He responded: 'The name of the game is freedom.' The audience was small but enthusiastic.

There was no programme, but he had learned that Tess Barlow was the reactionary woman. She was tall, skinny, and looked both dirty and underfed. When he introduced himself she said, with an American accent overlaying her natural Cockney, 'Potter, yeah, I was told about you.'

'I think Mr Race spoke to you.'

'That who it was? Look, I need a drink, a large whisky, d'you mind.' She downed it in two gulps, and he ordered another. She took his hand in one that was both predatory and slightly shaky, and led him to stools at the back of the bar. 'You like the play?'

'I didn't see all of it.'

'You don't have to say you like it, if I could be playing in legit theatre I would. You want to know about the Fetherby girls.'

'The Fetherby girls,' he echoed, in surprise at the plural.

They were close together on the stools. She smelled of

sweat, and something else that he could not place for a moment. Then he recognised it as marijuana.

'Yeah, it was Lenore I knew best. She was a wild one, do anything for kicks. Coulda been an actress, better than me, but still she'd never take it seriously, off with a new man or something, out to Saudi Arabia or wherever. Or got mixed up with drugs, knew her when she had a job as travel courier and was a carrier. Marvel is she never went in jail, but if you ask me drugs were mixed up in it.'

'Mixed up in what?'

'What?' He recognised with dismay a blankness in her look, one he had seen often enough in students high on pot or pills. And what a fool she was to start drinking when she was on drugs. 'You mean you didn't know?'

'Know what?'

'She's dead, Lenore is dead.' She fumbled in a scruffy handbag, and drew from it a clean envelope containing a well-preserved newspaper cutting. It was a half page from the *El Paso Daily Journal*, and the date was 18 December, rather more than two months ago. A news story headed *Death Fire in Chihuahua Hotel* had been ringed in red. The story, which ran to more than a column, said that two people had died in a blaze at the Obregon Hotel, Chihuahua, Mexico, and gave the names. One was Lenore Fetherby, the other Manuel Carrillo, who was described as a businessman. The cause of the fire was unknown.

'Gotta friend who knew Lenore, married some doctor who's half-American half-Mex, lives in El Paso now. She sent this to me, knew I was close to Lenore. I loved her, loved Lenore.'

She gripped his arm fiercely, yet the look she gave him had something calculating about it. Dudley's reactions were, he knew, incurably literary, and at that moment he could think of nothing but the line of Poe's that had so much delighted Rose Fetherby:

The sweet Lenore hath "gone before", with Hope, that flew beside.

But Lenore's fate did not concern him. He gave back the cutting.

'It's Annabel Lee I'd like to know about. I believe you

know her. She stayed with you in your apartment.'

'Yeah, right. But you got to understand —' She seemed to change direction in mid-phrase, as though she had forgotten what she had been about to tell him.

'Yes?'

'When you say apartment it's just a couple of rooms. All sorts of people kip there. But Lee, yeah, she was there. Not regularly, you understand, just a night now and then.'

'Paul Race said you told him she stayed last June.'

'June, yeah, that'd be about right.'

'That was when she still had her flat in Kennington.'

'I suppose. I didn't ask no questions, she told me whatever she wanted.'

'But you did know she had a flat in Kennington?'

'Sure, sure. I don't take notice of who lives where, you got to understand that.' A man whom he recognised as the revolutionary actor in the play came over and began talking to her in a low voice. 'Few minutes, Dave, see you in a few minutes,' she said. Dave raised a hand, drifted away.

'She's an actress too.'

'Yeah, that's right,' Tess Barlow said, without interest.

'You didn't know her well?'

'Right, that's right. Lenore was the one I knew. Loved her, loved Lenore. Lee, I didn't know her that well, but she stayed with me, that's it.'

'When was the last time you saw her? Lee, I mean.'

'What?' He repeated the question. She looked at him with little raven eyes that were not perfectly focussed. With apparent effort she said, 'This week.' He asked what day.

'How the hell should I know? Don't keep track of days, one's the same as another. What's today?'

'Wednesday.'

There was a pause, then she said triumphantly, 'Monday. Remember it was Monday because Monday there's no theatre, stayed at home in the *apartment*. There all day.' She glared at him. 'Lee came round. Wanted somewhere to sleep. Said no good, sorry, can't help, gotta couple friends staying. But she stayed, slept on the floor.'

'Was she with anybody?'

'No, on her tod. Just stayed, on the floor way I said, said

thanks, left in the morning.'

'Did she seem well? I mean, was she upset about anything?'

'How the hell should I know? People I know, they're all upset all the time.'

'And you've no idea where she was going? She didn't mention somebody named Wolfdale?'

The raven head was raised, and she spoke with surprising vigour. 'I never heard of any Wolfdale. Now I've told you what she said, nosey parker, and if you don't like it you can get stuffed. I'm off.' She rose on spindly legs, a little uncertainly, and pushed out through the swing doors.

On the way back to St John's Wood he considered what he had found out. Something about Tess Barlow worried him, but was his feeling anything more than the uneasiness experienced by the respectable in the presence of the erratic and unstable? He could see no reason why she should be lying. If Tess Barlow really had seen Annabel Lee on Monday there seemed no basis for his belief that she was either dead or in danger. Unless — but this was a possibility that he refused to contemplate — she had been involved in Wolfdale's death, and was on the run because of it. He could not get rid of the impression that there had been a further meaning in Tess Barlow's words, and that it was connected with the death of Lenore. She had died in a fire started by some unknown means. Was it possible that she had been murdered, and that her killer was also in pursuit of Annabel Lee?

When he got back Phyllis was in bed, but Steve listened patiently to his tale of what had happened.

'I never met Lenore, though she had the reputation of being a hell raiser. RIP Lenore. I don't see that her death's anything to do with her sister, or that you're any further on. Still, the essence of a wild goose chase is that you don't find any wild geese.' His features moved into the expression of solemnity that always seemed unnatural to him. 'I want you to know that I meant what I said in the office. Phyl and I have always envied you. There's an independence in the true devoted academic life that's — well, anyway, we envied you. And we still do.'

He could not help reflecting that any comparison between the opulence of this house and the frugality of his life at Graham would leave most people feeling that the envy should be the other way round, but he did not say so. Instead he remarked that Steve must have done very well out of the law.

'And publishing, my boy. Don't forget Otter Books, even though we've had our occasional problems. In this country, it often seems to me, enterprise is discouraged. Do you know what I say about modern England? It's a bankrupt American colony, kept afloat on North Sea oil.' He gave a bellow of true Steve laughter. 'I sound like Old Moore's Almanac. Let's have a nightcap.'

The restaurant was Italian. They sat in an alcove, a head of
Augustus Caesar behind them, separated from the nearest
tables by mock-marble pillars. The waiters sang in Anglo-
Italian as they moved around, juggling with trays. They wore
striped jackets and aprons, and had a convincingly Latin
look, although perhaps they all came from the East End.

'A pleasant little place,' Paul Race said. 'New, of course,
they spring up overnight like mushrooms. It's part of
London's changing face.'

'I haven't seen any changes that I'd call improvements.'

'You'll find the food here isn't bad. A little more varied
than the spaghetti of your youth.' Looking at the two-foot-
long menu Dudley saw what he meant. 'If Steve is to be
believed, none of you could afford anything except pasta
when you were students. He always talks as if those were
the happiest days of his life, and about you as a sort of
saint of unworldly scholarship. I was quite surprised to find
you existed at all.'

'It's the way successful men often talk about days when
they were short of money. If Steve ever actually
experienced academic life he'd die of boredom in a week.
I'm sure he's happy with what he's got, and he has reason
to be.'

'Perhaps you shouldn't believe everything you see.'

'I'm not sure what you mean. Steve told me last night
that Otter Books have had problems, but they surely can't
be serious.'

'He takes a lot of chances.' The young man's look was
troubled. 'It's not telling tales out of school to say so, since
he's mentioned business problems. Though that wasn't all I
meant.'

'You mean there are personal difficulties, too?'

Race hesitated. 'I think so, but it wouldn't be right for me
to talk about them. If he wants you to know he'll tell you,

and anyway, it's partly guesswork. But there's no doubt Otter Books is under-capitalised. Steve's looking round for a backer. That's public knowledge.'

'Is that why you're going to South America?'

The young man laughed, showing small, white, even teeth. With regular features, curly fair hair, ready smile, he was remarkably attractive, yet there was a suggestion of weakness and almost of effeminacy about the indeterminate mouth and delicate chin.

'No, no, I'm not fleeing the sinking ship or anything like that. The truth is, I'm not a very good lawyer, just a useful dogsbody.'

'Steve said you were wonderful at checking details.'

'There you are. Who wants to be good at checking details? I know Steve didn't mean it like that. He's been generous, given me a lot of encouragement, but I'll never be a first-class lawyer and I know it. I've got a farming background, though you might not think so.'

'Why not farm in this country?'

'Do you know how much you have to pay for land, the cost of stock, the Government restrictions? I know people who farm, and they spend a week of every month filling in forms. It's quite different in Brazil, I've got a friend who's emigrated. They recognise that livestock is the lifeblood of the country, and treat their farmers accordingly. I know it's not an ideal society, but from what my friend says they don't trouble foreigners, in fact they actually like them. I haven't made up my mind finally, though, I want to find out more about the farming possibilities before I do that. But I didn't ask you here to talk about my affairs. How did you get on with Tess Barlow?'

He listened carefully to what Dudley told him. 'I don't see why you feel any doubt about what she said. It sounds straightforward enough.'

'I don't know either. It was partly because she was high on drink or drugs, or a combination of the two. But there was something more, I don't know what. I felt the story she told me wasn't coming through straight.'

'She said she saw Annabel Lee on Monday. Do you believe that?'

'I'm not sure. I don't see what reason she could have had for lying, but — I don't know. I expect you think I'm foolish, pursuing a dream as Steve says?'

'Not foolish. Irrational perhaps. You're going by your feelings, and sometimes they're better than reason.'

Dudley ate the last mouthful of his saltimbocca. 'Tell me, Mr Race —'

'Paul, please.' The white teeth showed.

'Paul. Annabel Lee's next payment is in April, and then in June she's due to get the whole of her inheritance. What happens if you don't hear from her before April?'

'We shall hold the money for her.'

'And suppose that in June you get a request — in the form of a letter, say — that her inheritance should be paid to a Swiss bank account. In other words, suppose she hasn't reappeared in person by then. Would you act on the letter?'

'No, we should want authentication.'

'What sort of authentication? A sworn statement before a Swiss lawyer — or an Italian, German, whatever country she happened to be living in. Would that be enough?'

Race considered. 'Not as you put it. The very least we might accept would be a statement by the lawyer giving some independent identification of the claimant's identity. I don't think, though, that we should think even that was satisfactory. In the event of a claim from abroad, with Miss Fetherby not appearing in person but writing to say that she was too ill to travel or hated England and never wanted to come back here, or whatever you like to think of, then I imagine Steve or I would fly out to verify her identity and see that no trickery was being practised. But I hope you'll forgive me for saying that all this seems to me wildly unlikely. What makes you suppose she won't appear in London in June, and sign all the documents in our glorious new offices? I don't doubt that she has the date firmly in mind. You'll remember that she wrote from Graham asking that her allowance should be sent there. She may be eccentric, but she's not foolish.'

'I expect you're right.'

The restaurant, with its mock-marble columns, mock-casts of Roman Emperors, tessellated floor no doubt made of plastic, seemed to him for a moment wholly unreal. He looked at the bust behind Paul Race and saw, with incredulity touched with terror, that it was no longer Augustus Caesar but Nero. Was he losing his mind? Then he realised that the floor was moving very slowly, so that they had made a quarter-revolution of the room since they sat down. Paul asked with concern if he felt all right.

'I think so. I hadn't realised the floor moved. Did you find anything more in the papers?'

'There was something we missed in that quick look through, though I don't know it's of any importance. However, since you're going up to Yorkshire you may as well know it. I think we mentioned that Miss Fetherby inherited a cottage or house up there from her mother. It's not all that far from where Stewart Fetherby lives, as a matter of fact. I know Lee Fetherby used to go up and stay there sometimes, because we'd get a note at the office to say she was going up to the Kingdom by the Sea for a few weeks of peace, and we'd find her there if we needed to get in touch. I suppose it's possible that she's staying there now.'

'Did you say the Kingdom by the Sea?'

'Yes. That's the name of the house. Some sort of quotation, I believe.'

'That's right. The quotation comes from Poe, and it refers to Annabel Lee:

"It was many and many a year ago,
    In a kingdom by the sea,
That a maiden there lived whom you may know
    By the name of Annabel Lee."

Paul smiled politely. 'It's certainly an unusual name for a house, but of course Miss Fetherby wasn't the person who named it. That was done by her mother, and it came to her as part of the estate. It's at a place called Scarness, which used to be a village but has been partly eroded by the sea. The place was originally called Ivy Cottage according to the papers we have. Mrs Fetherby had it almost completely rebuilt, and renamed it. I've never been there, but I gather it's an eccentric kind of place, and certainly the rebuilding cost a lot of money. That was seven years ago.'

'Is there a telephone installed?'

'There is, and I have the number.' Steve had evidently not exaggerated in speaking of Paul's appetite for detail. He passed over a slip of paper. 'I haven't tried the number myself, because we really have no reason to do so, and it might be thought an intrusion. I've put another address on the paper. That's Mrs Waddington, who looks after the place, goes in and cleans it every so often, that kind of thing. No doubt she'd know if Miss Fetherby has been up there recently. I've sent her a line to say you might be coming up, but I've had a note typed just to give you official standing, as you might say. And here it is. She knows the firm, because we send her money every month.'

'That's very thoughtful,' he said, and meant it.

He had called Stewart Fetherby from St John's Wood on the previous night, after returning from Islington. The voice at the other end of the line had been brisk, and at first unwelcoming.

'Annie Fetherby, of course I know her, and her sister too. Haven't set sight on either of them for years, but from what I hear Annie's a rich woman now. What's your business with her, may I ask?'

He explained that he was a close friend, and had come over from America to try to find her.

'Come from America, eh? You must want to see her badly. And you say you're a literary man, publish books. I'll tell you something about Miss Annabel Lee, as you call her. She moves in a mysterious way and always has. Now that's a quotation you'll appreciate as a book man.' An enthusiastic snort came down the telephone. 'Don't see what you want with me, Mr Potter, but if you're set on coming up this way you're welcome to pay a visit. Come to dinner tomorrow, seven-thirty, and we'll have a drink before we eat. Mind, I eat at eight sharp. As a matter of fact I do have something here might interest you.'

He was in York by five-thirty, and rented a car for the drive to the Vale of Pickering where Fetherby lived. From his hotel room he tried the number Paul Race had given him, but got no reply. Then he dialled Elaine. A woman's voice answered, one he did not recognise. He asked for Mrs Potter.

'This is Mrs Potter.'

'Elaine. It's Dudley.'

Silence. Then she said, 'How did you know?'

'Know what? I called because I'm in York, and wanted to hear your voice.'

'Even though you didn't recognise it?' she said, sounding for the first time like the Elaine he remembered. 'It's your father. He had a stroke. I think he's dying.'

'Oh.'

'He's mentioned you several times recently. I'm sure he'd like to see you. But perhaps you won't want to see him. You were never one for facing unpleasant realities, were you, Dudley?'

The remark stung him. 'I'm glad you acknowledge the reality was unpleasant. Of course I'll come out. Tomorrow morning, if that suits you.'

She said, in the desolate tone with which she had first spoken, 'That will be all right. The doctor comes at ten-thirty, so make it eleven o'clock. And Dudley.'

'Yes?'

'I'm sorry if I sounded unwelcoming. Donald will be pleased to see you. So shall I. The address is 18 Hesdale Close.'

On the drive out through the suburbs of York, which with their trim bow-windowed, pebbledashed houses might have been the suburbs of fifty other English towns and cities, he thought about the past, about his father, about Elaine. Fifteen years ago the pattern of his life had seemed to be set. He had taken a first in English, was doing a post-graduate thesis on the minor Caroline poets, and looked forward without doubt to a successful academic career. He was engaged to Elaine, and she often came down to spend weekends at Woodlands, the solid suburban house in solid almost-suburban Sussex, quite distinctly a step up from a city suburb, with detached mock-Tudor houses instead of semi-detached pebbledash. In this world handsome Doctor Potter was a popular man. It was his father's popularity and

102

his easy gregariousness that Dudley remembered most clearly from his own childhood and adolescence, his father going out to bat for the village cricket team and taking the chair at the yearly dinner, radiating good fellowship and enjoyment as host at dinner and cocktail parties, comforting patients in distress, winning coconuts at a local fair and then giving them away.

Dudley had never shown any of his father's exuberance, and indeed had been intimidated by it. He was shy and retiring, sensitive like his mother as friends said. Lucille Potter was what the same friends called delicate, subject to nervous headaches that left her prostrate, reluctant to attend the functions to which she was invited as an appendage to her husband, an almost silent hostess at her own dinner parties. 'Lucille has all the sensibility, I've just got the gift of the gab,' her husband would say disarmingly, varying this sometimes by remarking that Dudley had the brains of the family, and no doubt got them from his mother.

Elaine, Doctor Potter would say, fitted into the family wonderfully well, and he couldn't wait for the day when he had a daughter-in-law. She had read economics, got a respectable second, and taken temporary teaching jobs, a couple of terms at a school in her native Yorkshire, and after that a job near London. It was not worth looking for anything permanent, because it was understood that they would be married when Dudley's thesis was completed. Then he would receive an appointment, and she would find a job wherever they settled. Elaine and Dudley had slept together only on that holiday in Devon with Steve Shilton, of which he had kept snaps. Had it changed their relationship, had it been somehow a disappointment for her, as upon reflection afterwards he supposed it had been for him? He had a long time to reflect on this, for a couple of weeks after their return from Devon the world in which he had been living ceased to exist.

It was destroyed by his mother's telephone call.

'Dudley,' she said. 'Your father has gone off.' Gone off, he echoed stupidly, what did she mean? He thought at once of curdled milk. 'He has left me. He has gone with Elaine.'

This was the incredible news that marked the end of the world.

There was more, of course, a great deal more. There were above all letters, streams of letters. They began with the traditional letter left by his father on the living room mantelpiece, and continued with the letter from Elaine which said that they would never have been happy together, that she and Donald had been irresistibly drawn to each other since they first met, that age made no difference, and that Dudley would be better off without her. And that was only the beginning. Steve wrote to Elaine and she back to Steve, his father wrote to Dudley apologising, asking for understanding, promising to look after Lucille. His mother wrote bitter letters to both lovers, and back came a sorrowful, self-critical, but somehow reproachful and self-justifying letter that they had both signed.

That was only the first wave of letters. The second included letters about resignation from the cricket club, giving up the practice, the question of divorce and a settlement for Lucille, pleas from Elaine about their desire to get married. The only person who wrote no letters was Dudley, who answered neither his father nor Elaine. He tried to dissuade his mother from continuing the correspondence with her husband, in which she pleaded with him to come back. He gave up the post-graduate course, devoted himself to seeing that the divorce went through smoothly and that his mother got an adequate settlement. When it was all over he looked for a job outside England, and found the one at Graham. It was not Oxford or Cambridge but it served his purpose, which was to get out of England, and anyway it was a good enough job. Just before he left, his father and Elaine got married.

His father told him of the fact in a chatty, cheerful letter. They had got married very quietly at a registry office in York, and he hoped to take up a practice just outside the city. The letter ended: *Dudley, old fellow, I expect you're still feeling pretty sore, but as Elaine says she and I were meant for each other from the word go, and it would never have done if she'd married you. As you know I've never been a man to bear a grudge against anybody, and I hope in this respect you're a chip off the old block. You'll be more than welcome here at any time, and I hope you can find it in your heart to send us your good wishes. Believe me, we'd both appreciate it.*

That letter too he left unanswered. He went to Graham, buried himself in a new world, another society. When his mother died three years later he did not return to England for the funeral, because he feared that he might meet his father. Over the years, as he knew, the wound had never healed, but like many aware of the nature of a psychological illness he found it impossible to attempt a cure. He had never become emotionally involved with any woman until he met Annabel Lee. The past had stayed with him for fifteen years. It was with some vague, hardly recognised idea that it would be exorcised through personal contact that he had telephoned Elaine.

Why was he going to see Stewart Fetherby, what did he hope that a retired supermarket owner could tell him? The nature of his relationship with Annabel Lee remained ambiguous, and it seemed to him that this ambiguity had its roots in her past, and that if he knew more about her childhood and adolescence the knowledge might offer a solution to her behaviour. Fetherby's words on the telephone about having something that might interest him contained at least the hint, the germ, the promise of something that might explain not her disappearance but her very nature. As he drove through mist and thin rain he repeated some lines of Poe's sad mysterious poem about a lost love. Was the sense of desolation he felt connected with the loss of Annabel Lee, or the impending death of the father who had been the idol of his youth and then the destroyer of his manhood? He could not be sure.

Brattick House was approached through an avenue of trees, and when this opened out into a courtyard he was surprised to see in the car headlights an elegant small Georgian house. For no good reason he had expected the supermarket owner to be housed in some eccentric Victorian Gothic structure. A single light shone over the front door topped by a handsome pediment. It was disconcerting to hear modern door chimes sound when he pressed the bell. The opened door revealed a stubby figure holding out a welcoming hand.

'It's Mr Potter from America. Stewart Fetherby. Come in, then, come in. Doris, where's that girl? There you are, Doris, take the gentleman's coat. And Mr Potter, you follow me.'

He handed his coat to a pert-looking snub-nosed girl, who gave him a look that seemed to measure him and find him wanting, and followed his host through three small unremarkable rooms that led into each other, to a similar one which contained a big television set, a three-piece suite, and some odd chairs and tables. A coal fire burned in the grate, there were pictures and photographs on the walls. What did the room remind him of, he wondered? And then realised that the suite was, in style and colour, almost a counterpart of that in the parlour at Rudderley Gardens.

'Seven-thirty to the minute,' his host said with satisfaction. 'I like a punctual man. I never have my first of the evening a minute before. seven-thirty, then ten o'clock on the dot I'm in bed. Punctuality, that's the thing, keeping to a timetable. You show me a man who keeps to a timetable, and I'll show you a man who's a success in life. What'll you take, Mr Potter? I can give you a fine single malt, smooth as a baby's bottom, which is what I drink myself. And, though it's a free country, I shall think the less of you if you spoil it with tap water. There's gin and vodka, but if you ask me nobody but a woman would drink gin and only a Russki would touch vodka. The single malt, is it? Good. And now, Mr Potter, what is it you think I can tell you about my niece Annie?'

The dim light from the two standard lamps showed Stewart Fetherby as a man with a round merry red face, and twinkling, but uncommonly sharp little eyes. While Dudley sipped the whisky which it had seemed inevitable he should accept even though he did not like it, he went into an account which omitted nothing. To provide a reason for his pursuit of Annabel Lee which might seem reasonable to a man like Fetherby, he said that they had meant to get married. The Yorkshireman heard him out without interruption.

'Remarkable story,' he said when Dudley had finished.

'You've never heard of this Wolfdale, you say. No more had I, never any word that she'd been married, though I'd not be surprised to hear anything about that girl. And you think Wolfdale had some hold over her? Might be so, but I know nowt about it. Last time I saw Annie was five years back, at Rose's funeral. She looked then as if she hadn't the least concern with the sad occasion. She and that sister of hers talked and laughed like it was a stranger in the wooden box, not her mother. Mind you, they were never close to Rose, but there are decencies you expect to be preserved. I'm afraid you've had a journey for nothing, Mr Potter. I'll say again that I don't know what it was you hoped I could tell you.'

'I'm not sure myself. I just feel Annabel Lee's disappearance is related to something in her past. I'm going tomorrow to look at a cottage she inherited from her mother. It's on the coast, at a place called Scarness.'

'Oh ay, Ivy Cottage.'

'Mrs Fetherby called it the Kingdom by the Sea.'

'She did a lot of daft things, did Rose, though none much dafter than your going out to look at Ivy Cottage. Just look at that table. What d'you make of it?'

The table, on which his drink stood, was a small circular pie crust affair, in what seemed to be dark oak or mahogany. He said he liked it. Fetherby tapped the table, producing a hollow, slightly reverberant sound.

'Plastic,' he said triumphantly. 'Admit it, now, you'd never know.'

'That's right. I wouldn't have known.'

'So why waste money on wood when plastic's half the price? Time for my second ball of malt. I take two each night before dinner, no more and no less. Join me?' Dudley said that he had to drive back, and declined. 'Come now, Mr Potter, you've got more in your mind than you've let on. What is it?'

He said truthfully that that was not so, and that he had to come up to Yorkshire to see an old friend. 'I notice that you use the name Annie. Was she generally called that?'

'Not on your life she wasn't. Rose hated it, called the girls by their full names, Annabel Lee and Lenore, and my word what a mouthful she made out of it. They were Annie and Lennie to me, and she didn't like it. "My daughter's name is Annabel Lee", she'd say in that mincing voice of hers. She was easily riled, was Rose, and it was a pleasure to rile her.' Stewart Fetherby's little eyes twinkled at the thought. 'If you ask my opinion she was half-cracked.'

'But she married a grocer.' He remembered his host's occupation. 'If you don't mind my putting it like that.'

'You say what you please. Stewart Fetherby made his money as a tradesman, and proud of it.'

'What about the girls, what were they like?'

'Annie and Lennie? They were good-looking girls, no doubt about it, real bobby-dazzlers when they dressed up. Wild though, both of 'em, took after their mother in thinking they were too good for the rest of us, never had any friends, not girls of their own age anyway. Lennie now, she ran off to London, then later was caught for thieving and sent to Borstal. Real scandal that was, I can tell you. Afterwards she never came home again. Horace put his foot down for once.'

'Tell me about your brother. I haven't got at all a clear picture of him.'

'Not surprised, he was always fuzzy round the edges.' The eyes twinkled again. 'He was a poor tool, Horace. The Fetherbys have been in the grocery trade for a century, Dad owned two shops in Halifax and we each got one when he died, fair's fair. I say that although he left Horace the best shop, even though I was seven years older. "Stewart", Dad says to me. "I want you to understand. You'll make your way in the world, fall on your feet wherever you drop. Horace is different". He knew it and I knew it, Horace had no go in him, he was always making the best of things and turning the other cheek. If he'd been a missionary out in Africa and the cannibals were getting him ready for the pot, he'd a' said we must remember the poor fellows don't often get a square meal. I was fond of Horace, mind, but it was no use thinking he'd make a success of anything. A few years after dad's death I've got a little chain of shops, Horace is just managing to tick over with the one. Quite contented mind, no complaints. I couldn't believe it, I just couldn't believe it, when I heard he'd up and married Miss Scudamore on the sly. They told nobody in advance, just went off and got married, came back and said we're hitched. Well, I says to myself, that's smart, there's more to Horace than meets the eye, but that wasn't the way of it. Shall I tell you what happened?' He did not wait for assent. 'The Scudamores always ordered groceries from his shop, had done for years. Horace delivered them himself, and one day Rose found him with a book of poetry in his van. Used to read the stuff while he ate his sandwiches, if you please. That was how it began, and it was a whirlwind courtship. What I mean, she courted him.' The snort of enthusiasm Dudley had heard on the telephone was evidently the nearest Stewart Fetherby got to a laugh.

'Was it a happy marriage?'

'Happy as most, I suppose. Marriage is a fool's game, if you ask me. Never tried it myself, never wanted to. No need for marriage to get a bit of grumble and grunt. You married? I know you were going to get hitched to Annie, but before that I mean? No? Wise man. You've had a lucky escape.'

'Were there any other children?'

'Just the two. I don't know how they managed it, Horace so dreamy and her nutty as a fruit cake. And a great joy the two children were to their parents, I don't think.'

'You've told me something about Lenore, but not about Annabel Lee.'

'You make a mouthful out of it, don't you? She was the older of the two, you know that. Went to the local grammar, so did Lennie, and from what I understood they got reports saying they were bright enough but didn't work, the trouble with all the young nowadays. Mind you, you should remember I didn't see 'em all that often, high days and holidays mostly. Annie was a good little school actress, I remember going to see her as Portia in that play about the Jew, *The Merchant of Venice*. Horace just sat back and said he was pleased, but Rose went on about a wonderful acting talent, she must go to drama school, that sort of nonsense. I believe she did go to some sort of drama school later on.'

'She told me about it, said it was a waste of time.'

'I'm not surprised. Otherwise, well, I don't know there's much to say. The young one, Lennie, had skedaddled by the time Annie had her acting success, if you call it that. She was in some other school productions too. Had a few boy friends, but I never heard there was anything serious, didn't do much school work. Pretty well as soon as she left school she was off to London like a shot, doing this acting course if that's what it was. Didn't hear much of her after that. She was like her mother, could put you down when she was talking if she felt like it, with that air of being surprised you were interested in vulgar things like making money. I said to her once, "I've got five shops when I had one a few years back, and I didn't do that by sitting on my arse", and she just opened her eyes and said, "Uncle Stewart, how clever of you", in a tone that made me want to put her over my knee and put a slipper to her b.t.m. And I'd have done it if she'd been my daughter, I can tell you. You want to know what they were like, just look at this.'

He went to a corner cupboard, took out a photograph album, and passed it over, pointing to a picture. Dudley's eye was first caught by the photograph on the opposite page, the first picture he had seen of Rose Fetherby. The face was long and thin, the eyes yearning, the lips bent in an uncertain smile. The shape of the face was unlike that of Annabel Lee, yet the expression was similar. The other photograph had been taken in a garden, and Rose was at the centre of it, sitting in a chair beside a table laid for tea. She had a strainer in her hand, and was looking as though uncertain what possible purpose it might have. Her smiling husband, standing beside her, was immediately recognisable as a milder version of Stewart.

Horace had an arm round each of the girls. One wore jeans and a shirt with lettering across it, the other a blouse and skirt, both had long hair. The girl with jeans had screwed up her face in a scowl, the other had put out her tongue.

'That's Annabel Lee,' Dudley said on a note of doubt, indicating the girl in jeans.

'Correct, that's our Annie. But you see what they both look like. Both behaving as per usual.'

110

'How old were they?'

'Fifteen and twelve, something like that. Before Lennie ran away.'

He looked through the album, but most of the pictures showed Stewart Fetherby himself, opening a shop, cutting the tape that marked a traffic-free precinct, making a speech at a dinner, dressed as a pirate at a fancy dress ball with Horace beside him as a lugubrious pierrot. There were other pictures of Rose, and two of Annabel Lee, one in school uniform and the other on a beach. They told him nothing. Why should he have expected that they would, when the most recent of them was fifteen years old?

Somewhere, as it seemed distantly, a gong sounded. Fetherby looked at his watch, and said with satisfaction that it was just eight o'clock. On the way to the dining room, Dudley asked whether his host lived here alone.

'That's right. Big place for one man, you'll be thinking, but I've got a position to keep up. I'm a magistrate, you know, school governor, all that sort of thing, wouldn't do to live in a tin shack. I'd sooner have a modern place, mind you, bang up to date, but they say there's more prestige if you've got something old. I give a reception twice a year, sometimes nigh on a hundred people. There's five acres of ground, most of it paddock, but a couple of big lawns. Have a man in to do it, of course, and living-in staff as well, that's Doris who keeps the place clean and does the cooking. Not many people can run to a girl living in, not in England nowadays, but I've never stinted on my comforts. If you've got the money why not spend it, I say. Look after Number One's always been my motto, because if you don't, nobody else will do it for you. Here we are.'

The dining table and spindle-back chairs were what he took to be reproduction Chippendale. Doris brought in plates of vegetable soup. Fetherby looked from her to the soup, eyes twinkling. After a couple of spoonfuls, he said, 'How d'ye like the furniture? Suits the room, people say.'

'Yes, it does suit the room.'

'Would you say it was the genuine old article, or modern, what they call reproduction?'

Surely this could not be plastic? 'Modern,' he said firmly.

111

'Very good modern.'

'Paper.'

'I beg your pardon?'

'This table and chairs, that side table over there, they're made of pressed paper. New process the Japanese have invented, won't chip, won't stain. Go on, feel it, run your hand over, try to scratch it. Can't do it, can you? Marvellous fellows those Nips, got the know-how on everything. Again I ask you, what's the point of paying hundreds of pounds, maybe thousands, for furniture, when you can buy this for a fraction of the money, and nobody can tell the difference? Doesn't make sense, but people still do it, there's a fool born every minute as the saying goes. What about Annie then, did she make any sort of name on the boards? If so we never heard of it up in Yorkshire.'

He could not bring himself to make a negative reply. 'She acts in fringe theatre. And she has played in America. She was in a play when I met her.'

'*Fringe* theatre, what's that when it's at home? Sounds like something on curtains. Any road, she doesn't have to worry now her mother's dead. Fallen on her feet right enough, has Annie. That's the best reason I've heard for marrying her. But you say money wasn't in your mind.'

'No, it wasn't.'

'And then she upped and left you. Typical. All you've told me is typical of the way those girls behaved. You're on a fool's errand, Mr Potter, the more I hear about it the more certain I am that's true.'

He got up, poured wine, rang a large brass hand bell (or was this perhaps also paper?) on the side table. Doris removed the soup plates, brought in a plate of lamb chops.

'What d'you call those, then?'

'I call them lamb chops.'

'Do you now? Give cook my compliments, and tell her they look like bits of burnt toast.'

Doris thumped vegetable dishes on to the table. She said to Dudley, 'Never guess I was the cook, would you, and he's just being sarky?'

'That's enough of that. You're here to serve, my girl, not talk to the guests. Don't you give me any cheek.'

Doris sniffed, and went out. The exchange was evidently not disagreeable to Fetherby, who kept an eye on the maid until she left the room. Dudley helped himself to vegetables, and sipped a sour red wine.

'You said you had something to show me that might be interesting.'

'Did I?' There was certainly malice lurking in Fetherby's little eye. 'Rose wasn't a hundred pence in the pound, you know that.'

'I'm not sure I understand what you mean.'

'A screw loose, not quite all there, lost some of her marbles. You have to bear it in mind. Mind you, she could manage her life all right, after a fashion, see the children went to school, look after Horace, but there was something about her — well, she wasn't normal. Didn't take any interest, no real interest, in anything except the old chamber pot.' He gave his snort at the look of consternation on Dudley's face. 'Chamber pot, Poe, that American writer. I must apologise for my sense of humour, it gets the better of me sometimes. Just look at the picture on the wall.'

It hung above the side table. At the centre of what looked like a swirl of blood-red draperies on the left, and iron blue ones on the right, was revealed a black cat, hair on end, large teeth showing. Behind the cat a ghostly figure in white knelt, with hands raised imploringly to an invisible deity. The figure's face was not entirely clear, but might have been that of Rose. The execution was crude, yet the picture had some effect because of the painful feeling evident behind it.

'She painted that, and a lot of others like it. After Horace died she started painting, and would you believe it, she put 'em all on show. Had to pay the gallery of course, but she sold quite a few of the pictures. I reckon it was mostly sympathy, though there were some people came up and wrote about the show, said she was highly talented. She gave me this one, I'd never have bought it myself. You reckon it's worth anything?'

'I don't know. It has some sort of power.'

'She said it was herself as Lady Ligeia, confronting the black cat that haunted her dreams. That was the way she talked sometimes. Does it make any sense?'

'Ligeia was the heroine of one of Poe's stories. She appeared in the grave where another woman should have been — only perhaps she didn't appear, it may be that the person who thought he saw her was deluded by taking opium.'

'Is that so? Too much for me, all that. Anyway, Rose had this show, it must have been a couple of years after Horace died, and she walked around as this Ligeia all dressed up in white. Annie came up for the opening, and *she* was dressed up too, as though she'd just come out of the grave, bits of what looked like earth on her clothes, except that they were all spotted with blood. She was supposed to be something or other in one of old chamber pot's tales.'

'The Red Death, I expect.'

'That was the name of it. All seemed morbid stuff to me, unhealthy, but it got in the local papers — Halifax they had the show, which was where Horace had his shop. I suppose it was good publicity, and maybe Annie thought it would do something for her acting career. I spoke to her, she'd been away from home a while then, and said to her what have you been doing, setting the Thames on fire, are you? She tells me she's working on a switchboard, a telephone switchboard. So much for all your grand ideas about going on the stage, I thought.'

'Lenore didn't come back for the show?'

'Not she. I don't think Rose had heard from her in a while. Annie was the one she liked best. She thought Lenore was a bad influence on Annie, though how she could have been when she left home so early is more than I can say. Ask me, Rose herself was a bad enough influence for any family. Some liver disease she died of, and of course she wouldn't see a doctor until near the end, didn't believe in 'em. I doubt if she'd seen Lennie since Horace died.'

'Annabel Lee said her mother had heard from her sister once or twice, saying she was in the Middle East and enjoying herself.'

'Maybe, I couldn't tell you. Far as I know the first time she'd been back for years was to her mother's funeral. There she was, made up to the nines and wearing a cherry red coat. "Hallo, Uncle Stewart", she says to me. "I've just come back to collect my share of the dibs, if any". If you wanted to say what was the difference between those girls you might say Annie was wayward, but Lennie could be downright vicious when she felt like it. But sweet as well, they could both make you think butter wouldn't melt in their mouths. There was a lawyer came up from London, pleasant young chap —'

'Paul Race.'

'Ay, that was the name. Lennie met him for the first time, and she was chatting him up. "Come on, don't make a secret of it, let's know the worst", she says. "How did the old witch leave the money?" Quite startled, he was for a moment. Then he says to her, cool as could be, that she'll just have to wait. Of course we were all disappointed, cousins and the like, and I thought Rose might have left a little keepsake to me, seeing I was Horace's brother, but not a bit of it. I should have known better than to think she'd do anything sensible. Only thing that made sense was that Annie couldn't touch the capital till she was thirty, and very likely that was put in by the London lawyers. Annie took it all calmly enough, and as for Lennie, when she found she'd got nothing she kissed her sister, wished her joy of the money, and said she was sorry she'd wasted her time coming up and she'd be taking the first train out of this dump. That was Lennie all over, Lennie and her cherry red coat.'

'She's dead now. She died in a hotel fire in Mexico, about two months ago. The cause of the fire was unknown.'

'In *Mexico*.' Fetherby shook his head, in seeming admiration of the Fetherby girls' capacity for travelling. 'In a fire. Cause unknown. And now you say Annie's disappeared. I'll tell you what it is, they're an unlucky lot, Horace's family. Mind you, those girls brought it on themselves, the way they went on.'

'But did they? Don't you think there's something strange about the cause of the fire not being known? As if a vendetta were being pursued against them for some reason?'

The other seemed to consider this seriously, then shook his head. 'I remember the will, which as I say was bloody silly, but if Annie died before she came into the capital then the whole lot went to the spiritualists. D'ye think they're pursuing a vendetta, as you call it, from the other world?' He laughed heartily. 'You're barking up the wrong tree. I told you Rose was nutty, and that could go for the girls as well. Imagine somebody going to live in that cottage, the way Rose did after Horace died. Nobody with any sense would have done that. Ah, here's the pudding. This is really something.'

The pudding was in a dish, under a large metal cover. Doris gave them plates, put down the pudding dish, said 'Hope you like it,' and went out.

'Come on then, lift the cover. It's a surprise for my guest. See what it is.'

Dudley raised the cover, and revealed a pile of manuscript. Fetherby gave his enthusiastic snort, took out a handkerchief and wiped his eyes.

'If you could have seen your face. You'll have to excuse me, my sense of humour does get the better of me. Sherlock Holmes played this same trick once, and that put me in mind of it. The fellow then had to be revived with brandy, but we'll have a glass of port. And a bit of Stilton to go with it.' He brought a cheese dish and plates on to the table.

Dudley's heart was leaping with excitement. 'Are they letters — documents — about Annabel Lee? These are the things you said would interest me?'

'Lord bless you, no. Why would I have any letters or papers about her?'

'Then what are they?'

'Ah, now we're coming to it. When I said something that would interest you, I meant as a bookman. And here it is.' He pushed the port along the table. 'My autobiography. The life and times of Stewart Charles Fetherby. I can tell you, this is a hard-hitting book. I've made some enemies in my time, Potter, in business and out, and there's few I haven't bested. This is going to sell like hot cakes in North Yorkshire. Look at it, man, it won't bite you. Take it off the dish and look.'

He took the mass of manuscript off the dish in a gingerly

manner, as though it were contaminated food rather than a disguised wild animal likely to take a nip at his fingers. The title page said *A Fighting Yorkshireman: My Struggle For Success* by Stewart Fetherby, O.B.E. He glanced at some of the chapter headings: A Boyhood in Groceries, My First Success, "Tha's Got Grit, Lad", Friends and Enemies, An Expanding Business, Scandals in Local Government, My Opinion of Women . . .

'Is there something here about Annabel Lee and her family?'

'Course there isn't, man. What d'ye keep harping on about that for? Horace is mentioned, but I told you this was my book. *Mine.*' A finger jabbed in the direction of his waistcoat.

'I don't quite see —'

'I'll tell you.' Fetherby downed half his port in a gulp. His face, the expression earnest, was pushed towards Dudley. 'I've tried this on the dog, given it to people around here, used to work for me and all that. They say it's tremendous, blow the lid off half Yorkshire. Then I send it down to some of these London publishers, and I get letters back saying it's of only local interest, or the style needs polishing.'

'I still don't understand. Why are you showing it to me?'

Now the finger jabbed at him, over and over. 'You're what they call a wordsmith, a bookman. I want you to read this. Then, if it's polish that's needed, you give it a shine, dress it up fancy. I want it published, the life and opinions of Stewart Fetherby, understand? And I can pay for it. I'll pay you for your time, and if I have to I'll pay for the publishing of it too.'

In his agitation Dudley found himself almost stammering. 'I'm sorry. This is really not — I can't help you.'

'You just tell me what you earn in a year, and I'll see you double it when this book's published.'

'I'm sorry. I don't do this sort of thing.'

'You won't read it, won't even look at it?'

'There would be no point.'

'No point, do you say *no point*? Then, by God, you can get out of my house.' An outstretched hand swept sideways, knocked over a glass. Red liquid slopped off the table to the floor. Dudley rose, making vague apologetic sounds. His host was roaring for Doris, but the roars merged into a coughing fit, so that when she appeared he was unable to do more than gesticulate, although the meaning of the gesture was plain.

'He's in one of his moods, then,' Doris said as she held out his coat. 'That book again. He gets into a state about it.'

'I'm afraid I made him angry. I don't like to leave like this.'

'Don't worry. I know how to quieten him down.' Her smile was slyly sexual.

Outside it was raining harder. As he drove back to York his tyres made a sucking sound, and lights gleamed up at him from roads that looked like wet rubber.

In the morning it was still raining when he drove to Orton, the village a few miles from York where Elaine lived with his father. Orton was a featureless village, a single street of small nineteenth century grey stone houses with three or four shops, surrounded by a rash of council houses and bungalows. Hesdale Close was part of this rash, a cul-de-sac of identical semi-detached bungalows arranged in a circle round a central patch of green turf. Little foreign cars, Japanese, German, French, nestled contentedly as cats beside the pavement or within integral garages. The car outside Elaine's bungalow was a Datsun Cherry, and the glass door had a mermaid etched in it. When he pressed the doorbell the chimes that sounded were identical with those of Brattick House. The door opened while the sound still lingered on the air. Elaine faced him.

It was recognisably Elaine, but his immediate impression was *how old you look*. That strained white face, the greying hair pulled back tightly from the forehead as if to emphasise the strain, the thickened figure — as his lips touched her cheek he thought that if they had met in the street he would not have recognised her. He looked round for relics of his father's past in the small front room to which she led him, but found none. No doubt it was natural that the new life should have contained nothing of the old. He asked what the doctor had said. She shrugged.

'It's a matter of time, that's all. Perhaps weeks, more likely days. There's nothing that can be done. I think he knows it himself. I told him you were coming, and he was pleased, but he's dozing now. I'll take you in later. I was going to make a cup of tea, will you have one?' She spoke in the hushed, conspiratorial voice used by many people in the presence of illness, and he lowered his own voice as he said that he would.

He stood and looked out of the window while she made

the tea, and thought that under no possible circumstances could he live here, even Rasputin Road would be preferable. Perhaps she sensed something of this, for when he turned from the window she said, 'It's not much, is it? We've been here three years, ever since the antique business folded up.'

'Antique business?'

'Of course, you didn't know. It was very difficult to get a medical practice. Donald went in with a couple of other doctors and they didn't get on, I think because he came from the south and they were both Yorkshiremen. So he bought an antique business, and we ran it together. He was always interested, don't you remember?'

He said yes, and it was true that he recalled his father naming the maker of a grandfather clock with an air of authority, and saying that this or that tallboy or whatnot was a fine little piece, but he had never considered such things as more than part of the air of authority and good fellowship that surrounded Doctor Potter. 'But it didn't succeed.'

'For a while we did quite well, but Donald was always too optimistic, bought too much. We were what they call over-extended, or we had cash flow problems. One of those financial diseases.' A ghost of the old Elaine showed in her smile. 'And then the recession finished us off. We had to sell up. It was a blow to him, emotionally as well as financially. I don't think he ever truly recovered from it. He often talked about starting up again, but never did. So we came here, and I went out to work as a secretary. He stayed at home and did the cooking, he turned out to be quite a good cook.' He shook his head in wonderment. 'Then a month ago he had the stroke, and since then I've been nursing him.'

'A sad story.' He said it without intending irony, but she flushed.

'You think you were hard done by, don't you? All right, you were, but it would never have worked. Us, I mean. We were wrong for each other, you must have known it. There was no, what do they call it now? No chemistry.'

'Chemistry,' he repeated. A ridiculous word to use, but perhaps it expressed something of what he had felt in relation to Annabel Lee.

'We've been happy, Donald and I, don't think anything else. No children, he thought he was too old, they'd be a burden on me. He was — is — always thoughtful.'

'Thoughtful for my mother? It killed her.'

'Oh, Dudley, really. She died of cancer.' He shrugged. 'I don't want to rake it all over, but theirs wasn't a good marriage, no matter what you think. Your mother was a neurotic woman.'

'I don't want you to tell me what my mother was.'

'All right. But I've said already, we were happy. Isn't that what two people should look for always? And he wasn't happy with her.'

Happiness, he thought, happiness. It seemed not the right word for what he had experienced with Annabel Lee, not intense or powerful enough. In those last sentences Elaine had raised her voice from the whispered monotone they had been using. Now she lifted her head like a hound pointing.

She went out for a moment, then returned and beckoned. At the door she murmured, like a nurse, 'Only a few minutes.' He felt a sense of relief, although very likely she had not intended to give the impression that this was an ordeal which would be only brief.

When she opened the bedroom door, emotion overwhelmed him. The figure in the bed, handsome regular features, mane of grey hair, ready smile, was immediately recognisable, and indeed seemed hardly to have changed. He wanted to embrace this figure, longed for the return of that old relationship with the father who had bowled to him in the garden, and had cried, 'Cracking good shot' as he drove the ball across the lawn into the flower beds. Then the man in the bed raised a hand, murmured his name, and he saw that he had nursed an illusion. The voice was thin and weak, the hand was raised with evident effort, what he had taken for a smile was a paralysis affecting one side of the face. He sat down beside the bed, took the strengthless hand, and spoke in what he recognised as the false voice the well use to the sick.

'Father, I never expected to find you in bed. But Elaine says the doctor's pleased with your progress.'

His father said, in the voice that he strained to hear, 'Good of you to come. Pleased to see you.'

'I had to come up to Yorkshire.' He recognised that any more of the truth about his visit would be unwelcome or irrelevant. His father said something he did not hear. 'What was that?'

'I said no need, no need to pretend. I know Elaine sent for you.' He started to say that this was not so, but behind his father Elaine shook her head. 'Wanted to explain, you see, never had a chance to explain.'

'There's no need.'

'Letters, you never answered my letters.'

'I know I didn't. I'm sorry.'

'You never understood. Behaved badly to you, both of us, especially me. That's what I wanted to say. Tried to write it, would have written it properly if you'd answered.'

'It doesn't matter now. It was all a long time ago.'

'A long time, yes.' A sigh, of sorrow or pain, came from the bed. The head shifted a little, the twisted face smiled up at him. The voice enunciated with ghostly clarity. 'How are you getting on?'

'At Graham? Very well.'

'Not here because — haven't lost your job?'

'No, no, nothing like that.'

'Come because Elaine said I was dying.'

'Of course not. I came because — to look up some manuscripts. For a book I'm doing.'

Were the words believed, were they even heard? The hand relinquished his, the head dropped. Dudley was aware of the sick room's antiseptic smell, and saw how thin was the arm inside the pyjama jacket. The head remained sunk, the arm lay motionless on the eiderdown patterned in small squares of blue and cream. There was a slight snoring sound.

He looked uneasily at Elaine. She said in a school-mistressy voice, 'Dudley's still here, you know. He's come specially to see you.'

The snoring ceased. The head moved up as though on a crank, inch by inch. 'Dudley, yes. Good of you to come.'

Must they go through that whole routine again, endlessly

perhaps? He gave Elaine a despairing glance, to which she did not respond. Then his father spoke in a clearer, stronger voice. 'I want you to forgive me, my boy. That's why I wanted to see you, to ask your forgiveness.'

He mumbled something. How was it possible to talk about forgiveness? Elaine was looking at him, the figure in the bed gazed upwards, one eye seeming larger than the other, the face fixed in that artificial smile. Suppose he said: 'You are the man and woman who have wrecked my life, so that I have been for years an incomplete human being. How can you expect me to forgive you?' But he knew he would say nothing of this kind.

'Dudley,' Elaine said questioningly. He shook his head.

His father began to repeat the words he had just spoken, but as he did so his face quivered, the words turned into an unintelligible mush of sound. Saliva dribbled from a corner of his mouth, and Elaine bent over to dab it away.

He said hastily, 'I forgive you. Of course I forgive you, if that's what you want. And Elaine too. But it's not necessary, I don't think about any of it now.'

He stopped. His father's eyes had closed, and he was snoring again. Elaine settled him more comfortably. Her eyes, as they met his across the bed, were scornful. She nodded to indicate that they should go back to the living room. There he lighted a cigarette for her.

'The doctor says he will probably stay like that, lucid part of the time, repeating himself, not knowing more than half of what's going on. He's sedated, not in any pain. I said it before, you've always been one for ducking out, haven't you? Don't worry, I'll excuse you, no need to stay around or to come back again. Not even for the funeral, if he dies.'

'I have to go back to the States.'

'Of course you have,' she said heartily. 'But what *are* you doing up here? You never told me. And you certainly didn't come to see him.'

'I'm looking for somebody.'

She puffed nervously at the cigarette. Had she smoked in the past? He could not remember, and lost himself in thinking about that Devon holiday. He supposed it was true that there had been no chemistry, no readiness to die upon the spot. He was startled when she spoke.

'Well?' The word dropped out of the air. 'From the tone of your voice it's a woman. You're not married?' It was more a statement than a question.

'No. I never married.'

'But it is a woman. Who is it you're looking for, and why?'

'Somebody I met at Graham. She left there suddenly and came to England. I don't know why, I think she was compelled to come. I believe she's in some sort of danger.'

'What's her name?'

'Fetherby. She came from Yorkshire, and I've been to see her uncle, Stewart Fetherby, but I got nothing from him.'

He spoke her name softly, as though it were a line of verse. 'Annabel Lee Fetherby.'

'I know her.' She stared at him and said accusingly, 'She's years younger than you. She was just a child.'

'You knew her? You can't have done.'

'Yes. You remember your thesis on John Cleveland — that famous thesis, was it ever finished?' He brushed away the question. 'I see it wasn't. I came up and taught here for a while. Annabel Lee was in my class. I remember her very well, the sweetest little girl, ten or eleven years old. Big blue eyes and pigtails, hated her name, and always wanted to be called Lee. There was a slightly dotty mother who came up to school two or three times, mad about mysticism and Edgar Allan Poe. Her mother wanted Lee to recite Poe's poem *The Bells* at a school concert, and there was a lot of argument. She did it in the end, but she really hated it.'

'Did you meet her father?'

'He was there, but I don't remember him saying anything, he was the original worm under foot. Funny little man, what was he called, Hubert?'

'Horace. What about the younger sister, Lenore? Did you see her?'

'She may have been at the school, but I had nothing to do with her. Lee was something special. There was a sort of sweetness about her, and she was a bit wafty like her mother. Intelligent enough, but gave the impression of being somewhere else part of the time. She was a good reader, and in the school plays. Of course they were only kids, but I remember thinking she was a good child actress.'

'She still does some acting. I don't think she takes it seriously.'

'She didn't take school seriously either.' She said suddenly, 'I saved her life, that's partly why I remember her. We were on a school outing, out in boats on Hornsea Mere. Do you know it? The biggest freshwater lake in Yorkshire, five miles round, and lots of little islands on it. The girls were playing about in boats, and one of them overturned. Should have been no problem, it was easy enough to cling on to the boat if you couldn't swim, and it wasn't for a couple of minutes that I realised a girl was missing. Then I dived in and caught her as she came up, gave her artificial respiration on the bank. It made the local paper, the only time I've been in print as a heroine. I told you about it at the time.'

'I don't remember.'

'Why should you? It wasn't important to you, I'm not sure anything about me was ever important to you. Your pride was injured, that's all.' He shifted uncomfortably, not exactly in denial. 'She must be, what, ten, twelve years younger than you?'

'Ten.'

'Are you going to get married? When you find her, that is.'

'I'm not sure, I doubt it. And it should be if, not when. Do you know anything about a cottage her mother had built, by the sea near Scarness? No, how could you, that was all much later. Mrs Fetherby came into family money, but she's dead now. I'm hoping Annabel Lee may be at the cottage. She owns it.' He stood up.

'You'll say goodbye to him.'

'I suppose so.'

They went again into the bedroom. His father's eyes were closed, his breathing shallow. Thin fingers moved uneasily over the eiderdown. With a distaste of which he knew Elaine was aware, he forced himself to bend over and touch the white forehead with his lips.

In the tiny hall she handed him his coat, and looked at

him with no particular friendliness as he carefully tucked in the scarf he had bought in London.

'If you'd known he was dying, you'd never have rung me, would you?'

'Perhaps not. But I'm glad I came.' He hesitated, then touched her hand. If there had been no chemistry in the past, certainly none existed now, but it seemed that he should say something.

'It's no use wishing anything for him, I see that. I hope you'll be all right.'

'If I'm not I shan't hold you responsible. After all, I never have. Good luck, Dudley.'

He said meaninglessly, 'Good luck, Elaine.' Then the glass door closed behind him. Outside rain was falling. He walked through puddles to the car.

And rain fell still as he turned off the main road, and went up through Cropton onto the moors. A thin mist blended with the rain after he passed Rosedale Abbey. Then there were no houses to be seen, nothing but the subdued browns and greens of winter heather on either side, and a few black-faced sheep who ignored him. Here at least was a world removed from Colonel Sanders and McDonalds who did it all for you, but was it any better? He got out to urinate, and his shoes squelched in the marshy ground. The car windscreen had misted over, and he sat inside for a couple of minutes with vision blanked out, wondering what he would find at Scarness. When he closed his eyes he saw her face, the body moving with invariable grace, heard the light laugh. He wiped the car windows and drove on.

Over Glaisdale Moor the mist thickened, so that he drove at no more than fifteen miles an hour. The same heather wound by like an endlessly repeated slow-motion film. As he left the moors and neared the coast the mist cleared but the rain intensified, driving straight at the windscreen so that he used the wipers at full speed. He almost missed the sign that said *Scarness Only*. There were pot-holes in the narrow metalled road which wound about like a snake. Scarness, when he reached it, was no more than a few dilapidated cottages and a garage with a sign that said

Petrol and Oil, and a poster: *All the Latest Model Fords in Stock*. There could be little market for them here.

The cottages were all at one side of the road. On the other a grassy slope led to the sea, churning away on rocks fifty feet below. Two miserable dogs barked unenthusiastically at him as he crossed to the slope and looked down. As he turned back a cottage door opened and a head popped out of it, topped by a mob-cap. It was years since he remembered seeing anybody wearing a mob-cap.

'You'll be the gentleman from London.' He agreed that he was. 'You'd best come in.' When he said that it was a wretched day she replied briskly. 'Yorkshire weather. We're used to it.'

He entered a tiny parlour where a fire burned in the grate, and every inch of available space was covered with mementoes of the sea. There were boats in bottles on the mantel, photographs of ships with naval ratings drawn up on the decks, pictures of a boat on a beach with a man standing beside it, others of what was presumably the local lifeboat and its crew, wearing sou'westers. Mrs Waddington followed his glance.

'Harry was at sea all his life. In the Royal Navy he was, then when he came out had his own fishing boat. You work with the sea, he used to say, and the sea'll work with you. But when he died seven years back he left nothing, so had the sea looked after him? Had it done anything for him? You'll take a cup of tea now, Mr Potter.'

'Thank you very much.' He had forgotten how universal cups of tea were in England as an accompaniment to conversation. This was the best he had been offered, strong and full of flavour. Mrs Waddington was a little wiry woman. She took the letter he had brought up with him, put on a pair of steel-rimmed spectacles and read it carefully, comparing it with the note sent by Race from London like an expert confirming the authenticity of a painting. Then she folded both letters carefully, and tucked them into a pocket of her apron.

'So what is it you'll be wanting, Mr Potter?'

'I hoped Miss Fetherby might be staying at the cottage.'

'She has been, but she's not. Leastways, not unless she's

back since Wednesday when I was last up. Wednesday and Saturday's my days. Why is it you're wanting to see her, if I may make so bold as to ask?'

He was unprepared for the gust of laughter with which she greeted his explanation. 'Disappeared, has she? I see you haven't known Miss Lee long. She's here today and gone tomorrow, always has been, and I never know when she's coming or going. Knock on the door there'll be, might be one this minute, and she'll be standing there and saying "Waddy, I'm in residence." Or maybe she won't even let me know, she'll be there when I go up to clean. Then, it might be a day or a month later she'll be gone, maybe leave a note and maybe not. Mind you, I'm not saying a word against Miss Lee, you can speak your mind to her and she'll not take offence. Miss Lee, I'll say, you know what you want is a husband, a man to look after you and stop your roving. She'd mostly just laugh at that, or say that's what you want, Waddy, not what I want. She's clever and yet she just isn't there all the time, if you take my meaning. Much like her mother. But it's a while now since she's been up.'

'How far is the cottage? I thought it was in the village.'

'Half a mile on. There's a road, but you'll find her muddy, and then there's another leads down to the cottage. More of a track, that is.'

'Somebody could come down the road from the other way without passing through the village?'

'Happen they could. Happen they have sometimes.'

'Did she, does she, stay there with friends?'

'That's the sort of question you've no right to ask, far as I know.' She repeated enquiringly, 'Not as far as I know. You're not her keeper. Or are you?'

'I'm hoping to marry her. That's why I'm worried.'

'The path of true love never runs smooth, they say, and it never would with Miss Lee. All right, now I know why you're asking I'll give an answer. Yes, she comes up sometimes with friends, no use asking me who they are because I don't know. Not for twelve months now has she brought anyone up here, far as I know.' He described Wolfdale. 'Never seen anybody like that.'

'When was she last up here?'

128

'Let me see.' She consulted a calendar. 'That's right, the end of October. And she must have had someone up with her then, come to think of it, because they left a real mess, I can tell you. Miss Lee was always slapdash, the way I said, but this wasn't just dirty crockery, there were things broken, a big old stone vase all in pieces, some plates and ornaments. And all of it left, none of it so much as swept up. I thought, next time I see Miss Lee I'll give her a piece of my mind. I don't mind clearing up, but this was more than that, a real mess.'

'As though there'd been a fight or a quarrel?'

'Could have been. But why should you think that?'

'No reason, really, except that it seems strange.'

'Ay, it was that. And it's not often she's away this long, not unless she's on tour. You know she's an actress, naturally you do.'

He said that he knew, while he reflected that for three months after October she had been with him at Graham, so that of course she could not have been here. When Mrs Waddington gave him the key she said, 'You've never seen the place. Has Miss Lee described it to you?' He said no. 'You're in for a shock. Miss Lee, she liked it, but I wouldn't stay there if you gave me a fortune.'

'You mean it's haunted?' he asked facetiously.

'I wouldn't mind a ghost. It's a crazy house, not natural. You'll see.'

A few minutes later he saw. A narrow winding road led out of the village and then became a dirt track, as if the road layer had lost enthusiasm for his task. The car bumped and squelched upward along it, with green fields on either side. Then he reached the top of the rise and stopped, astonished.

The dirt track led onwards, back to the main road. On the right it sloped down to a house standing almost at the edge of the cliff, a house like nothing he had ever seen. Part of the roof was marked by coloured slates set into a diamond pattern, in what he remembered to have read was a Yorkshire practice, like pargetting and tile hanging in Essex and Kent. This, presumably, was the original cottage roof. It was surrounded by four semi-circular metal constructions

129

that might have strayed from a science fiction film. He left his car on the track, and went down to the house by foot. Seen more closely, what had looked like metal shells proved to be brick, covered by some silvery substance which had been streaked and discoloured by rain and sea salt. They contained windows, some no larger than ships' portholes, but those facing the sea were big expanses of curved plate glass. The front door was a central sheet of coloured glass surrounded by the silvery substance. In a circle above, the name of the house appeared in faded Gothic script: *The Kingdom by the Sea.*

The door was no more than thirty feet from the cliff edge. He walked across, and stood looking down at the surge of water. A steep path wound among rocks and grass outcrops to the sea. When he went back to the house, the key turned easily in the lock.

The interior was like something in a science fiction fantasy. There was no entrance lobby. He stood in a room that had no inner walls, only heavy curtains in sombre reds and blues, invisibly suspended from the roof. The light was sepulchral and when he touched a button inside the door, concealed lights in the circular outer walls offered no more than a ghostly radiance. He remembered that Poe had detested glare, and had asked for a mild, or what artists call a cool, light within doors, with what the poet called con- sequent warm shadows. There were shadows here, either warm or sinisterly dark according to one's feeling. The furniture in the room was all low; tables, chairs and sofas rising no more than inches from the floor. All were in dark colours, the material heavy satins and brocades.

There were more buttons inside the front door. He pressed one, and an inner curtain drew soundlessly aside to reveal a bedroom. The bed was circular, the floor thickly carpeted, a dressing table with a circular looking glass contained a row of bottles. He recognised the scent Annabel Lee had used, a similar make-up to here, what looked very much like her brush and comb. Were these mere duplicates, put there to deceive him into detecting her presence? Could he reconcile the eccentric elaboration of these rooms with the girl who had packed all her belongings into a single suitcase? What appeared to be framed pictures on the bedroom wall proved to be texts from Poe. He read the Gothic script of one:

On Carpets.

As regards texture, the Saxony is alone admissible. A carpet should not be bedizened like a Riccaree Indian — all red chalk, yellow ochre, and cock's feathers. Distinct grounds, and vivid circular or cycloid figures, of no meaning, are here Median Laws.

The carpet on which he stood was a dark red, marked by golden curves that fitted Poe's prescription.

He shivered, returned to the door, and pressed again the button to close the bedroom curtain. Other curtains were similarly moved, so that when they were all drawn aside the whole place was revealed to him in what, he thought, a modern architect would have called open plan. It was smaller than it first seemed, no more than two bedrooms, the room he had entered from the front door, and beneath the original roof — not curtained but behind conventional doors — a bathroom and a modern kitchen. Their traditional quality emphasised the strangeness of the rest. It was not surprising that Mrs Waddington had called the house unnatural. He moved from room to room, not knowing what he was looking for, but finding nothing of a personal kind. A large wardrobe in the main bedroom contained dresses and skirts, but there was nothing he recognised. The kitchen, with cooking utensils neatly racked on the wall, showed no sign of recent occupancy. There were tins in cupboards, wine bottles in a rack, but the bread bin was empty and the refrigerator held only cans of soft drinks. It was true that Mrs Waddington's evident thoroughness would not have been likely to leave crumbs on table or floor, but there was something eerie about the absence of identity. It was as though the house itself had personality, not the person who had sometimes occupied it. He understood now more clearly what Stewart Fetherby had meant by saying that Rose had been mad, but not certifiable. The Kingdom by the Sea was surely the creation of somebody not entirely sane.

He returned to the row of buttons, and noticed a single small switch beside them. When he pressed it, tiny lights sprang out along the wall, illuminating five pictures. They were recognisably by the same hand as the picture in Fetherby's dining room, with similar swirls of dark colour, but in four of these paintings the swirls contained what might have been distorted faces and bodies, with skull-like heads and skeletal, very lengthy arms and legs. In two of the pictures a woman in white seemed to be running away from something unseen, mouth open in a scream of terror, her trailing dress caught by what might have been a clamp or a set of teeth. In the fifth picture the woman in white was looking up at a faceless figure painted wholly in purple, a figure bending over and enveloping her like a monstrous cloud.

The crude paintings gave a powerful impression of extreme unease, as if the painter knew herself menaced by some malign force. A ridiculous thought, but still it disturbed him.

The telephone rang.

In the silent house the shrill sound was terrifying. He began to shiver, then gripped one hand with another to control incipient panic, and began to look for the instrument. The sound seemed to come from the main bedroom, but no telephone was visible. He moved step by step through the room, like a child looking for something hidden who is told that he is now warm and now cold, until he had traced it to the circular bed. What was in or beside the bed? He moved aside the covering duvet, but found nothing. Beside the bed stood a low table with a large porcelain bust of Poe on it, the features severe, eyes unseeing. The sound seemed to be coming from this bust.

He wiped his forehead with his hand, and found it damp. Then he touched the bust, and found that what he had thought of as porcelain was papier mâché. He lifted the figure, and saw the telephone beneath. The shrilling continued. He picked up the receiver and said, 'Hallo.'

'Lee, hallo. This is Lee.'

The sound of that voice, light with its hint of laughter, brought her presence back to him painfully. He was aware that his own voice was a croak, unnatural.

'Where are you? I must see you, I have to talk to you.'

She ignored this. 'Now listen to me. Just listen and don't interrupt, okay?' A pause. He imagined her with eyebrows slightly arched, almost smiling.

'I left a note back at Graham, and I thought it was clear enough. "End of the affair", it said. Thought I'd keep it simple, since you're a professor and they're always looking for hidden meanings. But what do you do? You come over here, you start interfering in things that are nothing to do with you. I don't want that and I won't have it. The affair is over. I hope I'm making it clear.'

Below that lightness of tone he had always been aware of something hard as a steel spring, and he heard the hardness now. He tried to bring her back to reality. 'Wolfdalc's dead, do you know that? And the police want to talk to you. I have to know what's going on.'

She interrupted him during the last sentence. 'I'm told you're worried, got some idea that I'm in trouble, might be dead even. Well, I'm not dead, and if there's any trouble I'll get out of it without your help. So be sensible, Lee, and go back where sensible professors belong, teaching their students. Just think how they must be missing you.' She softened this with her characteristic laugh.

'That doesn't matter.' He summoned up all the things he thought and feared. 'I believe you're somehow being forced —'

Again she broke in. 'Have I said it loud and plain enough? Stop interfering. Forget me. I mean it.'

'I can't do that. I want to see you, I want you to tell me what you've just said face to face. Where are you now?'

'Goodbye, Lee.' A pause. A click. The connection was broken.

He sat on the bed, head in hands, thinking about what had been said. Had there been a note of constraint in her voice, as though she was being forced to say the things she did because somebody else was there, somebody who was threatening her? He could not truly say that he had detected anything of the kind. Yet there had been something strained, artificial, *wrong*, about the conversation.

What was it?

He had been sitting for what seemed minutes before he understood that what worried him was the click with which the call had ended, a sound that had come before the breaking of the connection. He tried to recall every word spoken. Had there been a conversation at all, or had he been listening to Annabel Lee's voice on tape, with pauses left to give an impression of naturalness? He could not remember any point at which she had replied to a remark, or even made an implicit comment on his words when she spoke again herself. If it was a recording then it must have been made under duress, and it was probable that she was no longer alive. But as he sat on the bed another possibility occurred to him, one he could hardly bear to contemplate.

Before driving away he examined the track outside the house for signs indicating that another car might have been there in the past few days. He saw no marks of tyres, nor any footprints except his own, and what were no doubt Mrs Waddington's boots. There were questions he must ask Mrs Waddington before he went back to London, although he did not expect conclusive answers. He stood on the cliff top, looking out again at the rocks below, the slippery path leading down, the water constantly curdled to anger. Then he walked up the green slope to his car, and left the Kingdom by the Sea.

'Darling Dud, I told you it wasn't a good idea to see Elaine. It *never* does any good to hark back, haven't I always said so, Steve?'

'Stop pestering the man, Phyl. He looks flaked out.'

'I'm all right,' he said, although it was true that the trip to Yorkshire had left him drained of energy, as though recovering from an illness. 'As a matter of fact Elaine remembered Annabel Lee. She taught her long ago, when Elaine did that stint up in Yorkshire.'

'Sorry to hear about your father.' Dudley waved a hand, hardly knowing what the gesture indicated, perhaps just an unreadiness to talk about his father's illness. 'Did you see Fetherby, and was it a total waste of time as I said it would be?'

'I saw him. He's an awful little man, but still he may have told me something useful.' Steve waited, but he did not elaborate.

'And you went to the cottage. What about that?'

'It was extraordinary. Frightening, too.' He told them about the telephone call, but not of his suspicion that it might have been recorded. Phyl nodded with an appearance of satisfaction.

'I told you she was a bitch. That's it, then. All over.' She came across and kissed him. 'We'll have a *lovely* party tomorrow, and then whenever you want to you can go back and forget the whole thing.'

'I'm not so sure that Dudley wants to do that. I remember that look on his face from of old when he was being told things he didn't like by some dry-as-dust tutor, a kind of "You've explained Milton to your own satisfaction but not to mine" look. Am I right?'

'I don't know,' he said truthfully. 'I really don't know.'

'Another thing. That policeman, what's his name? Bleek. Rang up, wanted to know where you'd gone, when you'd be back. He's coming round at ten tomorrow morning. Any idea what he wants?'

'None at all, unless it's to report progress.' He looked at Steve, and Steve's Punch-like face looked smilingly back at him.

Bleek arrived on the stroke of ten o'clock. They talked in Steve's study, a small room on the first floor. One wall was covered with photographs which almost constituted a life history, beginning with Steve as a baby, moving on to show him an open-mouthed but even then powerful-looking small child standing for some reason on a chair, schoolboy with cap on back of head, and student at a Rag Day. Here Steve, dressed as Cleopatra and looking remarkably womanly in spite of his aggressive nose, beamed at the camera, and Dudley as Harlequin stood by his side. These were succeeded by Steve gowned as youthful lawyer, Steve and Phyl on their wedding day, Steve behind the black and white desk in his office, standing with arms folded before the Otter Books stand at some book fair. To his surprise Bleek showed interest in the photographs.

'This is your host, Mr Shilton, right? Quite a high flyer from what I hear.'

'I don't know what you mean.'

'Why, you see his name everywhere. Lawyer turned publisher, unusual combination. This firm of his, Otter Books, I hear they're expanding, looking for new capital, you know about that?' He shook his head. 'Of course if he doesn't get it — but money breeds money, as they say, and if you owe a million to the banks they'll always lend you more for fear of losing what they lent in the first place. Hard for a simple policeman to understand, the games clever people get up to, quite legitimately of course. Hard for a professor too, I daresay. And my word, here you are too, all dressed up. You haven't changed much.'

'Thank you.'

'It's the sheltered life you lead, no doubt. Don't see much of the nastier side of things. Educating the young for the permissive society, that must be very congenial, though of course we're the ones who have to pick up the pieces when those permissive boys and girls grow up and go about robbing and mugging and murdering.' Bleek's thin face seemed today to be thinner, the corners of his mouth were permanently turned down as if he had tasted something disagreeable. 'What have you got to tell me, then? I heard you've been up to Yorkshire looking for your Miss Fetherby. Did you find her?'

'No.'

'Nor any indication where she might be?'

'I'm not sure. I spoke to her, or at least heard her voice.'

Bleek listened attentively to the story of the telephone call. 'You're sure it was her voice, not a good mimic?'

'I can only say it sounded like her. And whoever spoke knew what she'd said in her goodbye note.'

'And this idea of yours that you heard a recording, and it wasn't really a conversation at all. How certain are you of that?'

'Not certain. The final click put it into my mind, a separate click before the receiver was put down, but I can't be sure now that I really heard it although I believe I did. I've been over the whole call in my mind twenty times, trying to remember the exact words. It seems to me there were no direct responses to what I said, but again I can't be quite sure.'

'Your conclusion would be that somebody wanted to make you think Miss Fetherby was alive when in fact she's dead. But if the recording is genuine it must have been made voluntarily.' Dudley did not reply. Bleek said sharply, 'You're not holding anything back, I hope, Mr Potter? That wouldn't be helpful.'

'I've told you all that happened. I still don't know why you wanted to see me.'

The policeman seemed to consider the question. Dudley sat behind Steve's writing desk, which was bare of papers and ornaments. Bleek was opposite, in a chair that was a little lower so that Dudley should have had an advantage in looking down at his companion. In fact, however, Bleek's height meant that he sat up in the leather chair (no plastic furniture for Steve) so that they were at eye level. The effect was slightly menacing.

'I told you there was a possibility Ira had been killed at

the orders of one of the big boys. This would probably have been somebody outside this country, a contract put out in Holland or West Germany. They wouldn't have liked it if they'd known Ira's little arrangement with me, they don't understand that kind of thing. I also said against that idea, that if they'd put a contract on Ira they'd have been likely to make it conspicuous, a warning to encourage the others as you wordsmiths put it. I've put out a few enquiries, and it seems there was bad feeling between Ira and a Dutch gentleman named Doig Merck, something to do with Ira pulling Merck's girl when he was in Amsterdam with one of his theatre groups. He was there on business, you understand, but when a piece on the side was offered he wasn't one to say no. My informant tells me Merck was very peeved, and of course if he was settling a private grudge he might quite likely have wanted to fix it so it looked like suicide.' Bleek looked gloomily at his fingernails. 'What you do in the way of business is one thing, a private grudge is another.'

'So you think Merck ordered Wolfdale's killing?'

'It looks that way. The lad who handles things for Merck over here is named Dai Davies, a cute little bugger of a Welshman who's going to be too smart for his own good one day.' It would have seemed impossible for Bleek's mouth to turn down further, but he managed it now, so that the thin lips formed a crescent of disapproval. 'On his payroll Dai has an East End Jewish boy called Puffball Nathan, I don't need to tell you why.' Dudley shook his head. Bleek said with no sign of amusement, 'Because he specialises in blowing people away. Now, Puffball hasn't been seen around for the last few days. Why not? Because he's got himself a new bird and taken her to Torremolinos or Rimini or wherever's the place Puffball takes the birds he pulls, and he pulls quite a few, or, and this is the story on the grapevine, Dai's told him to keep his head down because he blew away Ira.'

'So that's what happened? Annabel Lee had nothing to do with it.'

'Did you hear me say that? You didn't. I'm telling you what I hear, no more than that. Point is, it suits us to believe that's the way it was, do you read me?'

Dudley hesitated, and said he didn't. Bleek's sigh was elaborately patient.

'I told you before, Ira gave us a lot of useful info, though I don't doubt he kept his mouth shut when he wanted to. He leaves a hole, and I want to fill it. If we go along with the story that was fed to my lad who's been asking around, then we have the chance of planting somebody to take his place without too much fuss and bother. Those silly old b's at Scotland Yard will believe anything, Merck'll think, maybe he'll even believe Ira wasn't a grass and wipe his eye because there's a good man gone for nothing. There's a laddie lined up now to replace Ira, a right villain in the rag trade — because of course the theatre game's all up for the time being, Merck'll know that. But if we start breathing fire and let it be known Merck had found out Ira was a stoolie and put out a contract on him, we'll set alarm bells ringing. And alarm bells ringing is something we can do without.'

'But anyway, Miss Fetherby had nothing to do with it?'

Bleek leaned forward and for the first time showed animation, in the form of annoyance. 'Don't you understand I'm saying it doesn't matter how Ira was killed? I'm telling you the way we're playing it, that's all. I've got an operation to worry about, and it's the operation that matters. I don't give a tinker's, if you'll forgive the old-fashioned way of putting it, who killed Ira Wolfdale. I just want you to stop poking your nose in any further, because if you do then it'll get chopped off. If Merck and his friends don't do it, I might.' The mouth corners turned upwards. Was this Bleek's idea of a joke?

'I'm going back to America. To my college.'

'An excellent idea.'

He said wonderingly, 'And you really don't care who killed Wolfdale? It doesn't interest you?'

'Of course it interests me, if you put it that way. Other things are more important, that's all.'

'Can you tell me at least whether you found any trace of Miss Fetherby in the flat.'

'Why, yes. Yes, we did.' Bleek again contemplated his

beautifully-kept nails. 'She was at Malcolm Court. She probably stayed the night.'

'How do you know she was there?'

'A woman in another flat saw somebody answering Fetherby's description, medium height, fair, casually dressed, with Ira on Sunday night.'

'You don't know it was her. The description would fit hundreds of girls.'

'Fair enough. But Mr Race was able to provide us with a photograph from the files, though it's three or four years old. The woman said it looked like her, though she couldn't be sure. Here's a blow up.'

It was a casual snap taken in a garden. She was wearing a dress he had never seen, and the blow up was grainy, but there was no doubt the photograph was Annabel Lee. 'You couldn't base a firm identification on this.'

'There was something else. We found it in the dustbin torn into small pieces, and it's been put together. This is a photostat.'

He found himself looking at an airline ticket, the joins showing where it had been pasted together. It was in the name of Ms A.L. Fetherby, one way, London to Johannesburg. The ticket was dated for Wednesday, and it was now Saturday. He said stupidly, 'This was torn up.'

'Correct. Of course another ticket could have been issued, but it wasn't. We checked. We checked other flights too. There's no record of a Miss Fetherby flying to Johannesburg on Wednesday, or any other day this week. One scenario could be that she stayed Sunday night with Ira. Somebody did, Mr Potter, no use looking injured, there were semen stains on the sheets. Maybe she was going to Jo'burg with Ira, changed her mind and tore up the ticket to show she wasn't going. Maybe he found the ticket, tore it up himself and said you're not leaving England. None of it proves anything, nor does the shooter. It was a Colt .38, number filed off, easy enough to get hold of these days either here or in the States. But all of it's conjecture, no need to worry about it being proved.'

'What I worry about is that she's being kept prisoner, and whoever's got her forced her to make that call to me — or the recording if it was that — to show she was still alive.'

'And then killed her? Or had they killed her already? It's got more holes than a colander, that idea. If I were a betting man, Mr Potter, I'd say somehow or other you were being played for a sucker, though I don't know who's doing it or why. But I could be wrong, it's happened before.' He got up, stretched, went over again to the photographs. 'Nice to keep up old friendships. You and Mr Shilton, I mean.'

'We were at college together. I haven't been in England for years, but we've always kept in touch.'

'No friend like an old friend, they say. But still, if I were you I'd get back to the States where you belong. Leave investigations to the professionals, they're used to it.' He nodded, and was gone.

Two minutes later Phyl came in with coffee. She complained that she had missed the chance of talking to a real policeman. 'It's of the *wrong* things about middle-class life, Dud, that we never meet real people. Would you say a policeman was a real person?'

She was wearing a padded pink housecoat, and he was aware of her lush attractiveness, even though it presented no temptation to him. Aware also that she presented herself as silly, when in fact she was shrewd.

'I'm not sure it's the right word for this particular policeman. He told me it was a good idea to go back to the States.'

'There you are then.'

'And he seemed interested in Steve.'

'*Did* he? In what sort of way?'

'He seemed to think Otter Books might be over-extended, or whatever the phrase is Rosemary quoted the other night. Looking for money.'

'Darling, aren't we all? Steve doesn't confide in me about such things, we're not truly a confiding pair.' She sat in the chair Bleek had occupied. Her red-stockinged legs emerged from beneath the housecoat. 'In fact I'm not sure we *are* a pair if you know what I mean. But I have every confidence in Steve over money. I think he's got hold of some new partner who's got pots of the stuff.'

There was a tap on the door. The girl he had seen on his

arrival put her head round it and said Doctor Bruxley was on the 'phone. Phyl got up.

'There's nothing wrong with Rosemary?'

'Oh no, Bill's just a friend. You'll see him tonight. Darling, we are looking forward to it, it's so *good* to have you here. I wish you were staying for ever.'

The rest of the day passed — how did it pass? He thought about the telephone call in that unnerving house, of the house itself standing on the cliff edge with the sea raging below, about what he had learned from Mrs Waddington after leaving The Kingdom by the Sea, and what Mrs Morris and the junk man Crundall had told him. It all seemed to lead to a logical conclusion, although if he accepted the conclusion it did not tell him where Annabel Lee was now, or even whether she was alive.

In the afternoon he went for a long walk past Lord's, through Regent's Park to the Zoo. There he contemplated polar bears, lions, monkeys, and wondered which he most resembled. One might wish to be a polar bear, remote from the rest of the animal kingdom, at home in "thrilling regions of thick-ribbed ice", one could aspire to being a King Leo, proud, angry and contemptuous of compromise — but it turned out that most of us were undoubtedly monkeys of one kind or another, lemurs, gibbons sad, breast-beating gorillas, feebly lecherous and weak, at home only with the chatter of our kind.

He returned to find Steve home early, and preparations for the party in full swing, with a waiter and two maids called in for the occasion. Champagne would flow, there was to be a buffet in the dining room, eighty or a hundred people were expected. He expressed astonishment and gratitude to Steve, who waved the words away.

'Nonsense, Otter Books are picking up the tag. It all promotes the image.'

'Steve, ever since I arrived I've been hearing things at second or third hand about Otter Books being in some kind of trouble, even though the word itself is never used. Today it was the Scotland Yard man nosing round the idea. Is it true?'

They were in Steve's dressing room, and he was considering shirts. 'Do you like this?' It was in mauve and purple stripes. When Dudley did not reply, Steve burst out laughing. 'Too loud for you? Handmade though, you won't see more than a dozen like it in London. If you'd asked me that question a couple of weeks ago I'd have had to say, well, I'd have said things are dicey, we may have over-reached ourselves a bit, published too much too fast. Now, Dudley lad, I'm happy to tell you that problems are solved. I have taken unto myself a partner, one Sir Leslie Garrity, Bart — yes, a man with a handle to his name, as we used to say in the good old bad old days.'

'He's the man Phyl said had pots of money, I suppose?'

'A very fair description. Leslie had money inherited from his villainous jerry-building father — you've been out of the country too long to know of Garrity Estates. He longs to be connected intimately with a publishing firm, I have a publishing firm and wish for intimate connection with what, again to go back to our youth, we used to call the green stuff. Doesn't that sound like a perfect relationship? Well, not perfect perhaps, but Leslie's harmless, and he's providing the essential blood transfusion of cash.'

He put on a purple velvet jacket and trousers. Dudley became alarmed.

'You know I've only got the suit I came over in, apart from this jacket and trousers. I'd have brought something if I'd known —'

'Think nothing of it. It's not a grand party, just that I like to look like a peacock, as Phyl will tell you. She says the vanity of women is nothing to that of men. Why don't you take a bath, put on your perfectly nice American suit, and let your natural goodness shine out. And don't worry. If you have a fault it is that you worry too much. Just lie back and enjoy it, as the old folk proverb advises.'

When he came downstairs an hour later the first guests had arrived. He was relieved to see that most of them wore perfectly ordinary suits. There were even a few in jeans and casual jackets who might have been Graham students. Phyl wore an emerald green dress that revealed her powerful shoulders. She held out to him hands dripping with rings.

'Dud, this is Bill Bruxley, that is Dr William Bruxley. Bill, this is our very old and dear friend Dudley Potter, over from the States.' With the introduction made she left them.

Dr Bruxley was a handsome man in his forties, whose grey-tinged hair curled naturally. His smile had the ease of long practice.

'Steve and Phyl have talked about you so often I feel I know you already. Are you here on a sabbatical? You see I know the language.'

'Just a short holiday. Is your practice local, Dr Bruxley?'

The smile broadened to show splendid teeth. 'I'm not a family doctor, I have a psychiatric clinic. And I have the besetting vice of psychiatric experts, I write in the press. I even write books. I'm an Otter author.' Before Dudley could ask the title of the book, Bruxley told him. '*Know Yourself Through Psychiatry*. Now in its third printing.'

'Congratulations.'

'Difficult subjects discussed in simple language. All the things you wanted to know about psychiatry and yourself, but were afraid to learn.' Was Bruxley quoting from his own blurb? He escaped on the pretext of getting his glass filled, and made his way across the room to Rosemary, who stood by the door looking miserable. She held a glass of bright red liquid.

'Tomato juice,' she said. 'They say I'm too young to drink champagne. Geraldine's people gave a party and let her drink anything she wanted. She had six Bloody Marys, that's vodka and tomato juice.'

'I hope that isn't — '

'Silly, I told you it was tomato juice. I wouldn't mind, but it's so childish, as though I'd never had a drink in my life. What happens in America? Do people of my age drink?'

'Coke or root beer, I suppose. That's non-alcoholic.'

'I know what root beer is.'

'Perhaps some wine. But not hard liquor, not vodka or gin.'

'I thought America was up to date. He's screwing mum, you know.'

'What did you say?'

'That creep you were talking to. Mum and Dad have awful rows about it. They think I don't know. People are so stupid.' She grimaced at her glass.

'Are you sure of what you're saying?' He added harshly, 'Even if you are, you ought not to talk about it.'

'Everybody does it. Geraldine's father keeps a woman in a Pimlico flat, Geraldine says it costs him ten thousand a year. People make me sick. I mean, why don't they just say what they're doing, why not let everybody know, what does it matter?'

She looked down at the golden carpet as though about to cry. He did not know what to say.

'Rosemary, don't worry. You might be mistaken.'

'Of *course* I'm not mistaken. I'm going up to my room, I hate this party.'

The girls moved around with champagne, the room filled up. At the other side of it he saw the small delicate features of Paul Race, but otherwise he recognised nobody except his hosts, and why should he expect to? He was about to push a way across to Race when he felt a light touch on his arm.

'Mr Potter? Steve's told me all about you, so I hope I may introduce myself. My name is Garrity.'

Sir Leslie Garrity stood no more than a couple of inches over five feet. His complexion was sandy, his appearance inconspicuous. He wore rimless glasses.

'I expect Steve has mentioned that we are going into partnership. I count myself lucky to be taking part in such an exciting enterprise, and to be in association with Steve. He has such — such vitality, don't you think? To make the shift from law to publishing, isn't that amazing?'

'Amazing.'

'I don't think I should be overstating the case if I said that Steve is one of the most remarkable men I have ever met.'

'Remarkable.'

'He's spoken of you in the very highest terms.' There seemed no possible comment on that. With a touch of archness Garrity went on. 'And he mentioned your youthful project.'

'Our project?' What had Steve been saying?

'The story of the banger. A wonderful idea. This is not the place to talk business, but if you think of writing the book I should be eager to commission it.'

The History of the Banger: it dated back to their student days, and had been one of Steve's typical semi-serious ideas. They would visit a selection of the English pubs that sold hot sausages at lunchtime over the counter, and grade them according to taste, meat content, spiciness, and any other category they could think of. They would compare home-made bangers with the factory article, and — this had been the core of Steve's brainwave — they would get a sausage manufacturer to put up a prize for Britain's best sausage and, if this proved to be home-made, the manufacturer would guarantee to make an identical article. Of course they had done no more than eating dozens of bangers in different pubs and making a few notes. What kind of idiot must Garrity be? But he had not stopped talking.

'Steve's mention of it was casual, but it caught my imagination at once. And of course we can extend the field of investigation to the States. *The Banger, English versus American*, what about that for a title?'

He shook his head dazedly, doubtful whether Garrity was in his right mind.

There was a clapping of hands. Voices were more or less stilled. Steve appeared above the throng, standing on a chair, the purple and mauve stripes of his shirt brilliant under the lights, his red face shining. His voice retained the fine resonance of his youth.

'The best parties are those that have no speeches, and this will be one of them. No speech, just a couple of sentences. This party is a welcome home for Dudley Potter, an old and dear friend of mine and Phyl's, whom we haven't seen since student days. Dudley, I raise my glass.' Dudley raised his own, and sipped. A murmur, perhaps of appreciation, was quickly stilled by Steve. 'Second, the party is to announce the expansion of our Otter list, and to say with what pleasure I welcome as a director and working partner my friend Sir Leslie Garrity. Leslie, will you step this way?'

Flashlights went off as Garrity reached his partner, stood on another chair and, with Steve towering over him, shook hands. He then said something of which only the words *co-*

operation, *expansion* and *privilege* could be heard, before he was drowned by the wave of sound as full conversation returned. Dudley found himself next to Paul Race.

'How did it go up in Yorkshire? Did you find anything useful?'

'I'm not sure.' He told the young man about the telephone call, and his suspicion that it had been recorded.

'But — forgive me for saying so — if you're in no doubt that it was Miss Fetherby's voice, shouldn't you perhaps do what she asked and give up looking for her?'

'I'd come to much the same conclusion. I'll be talking to a friend at Graham tonight if I can get through, and I shall go back next week, although I don't like leaving questions unanswered. Did Bleek tell you that he thought Annabel Lee had stayed at Wolfdale's flat, and about the airline ticket?'

Race nodded. 'He saw Steve with me, and told us both. Then I found the photograph in the file and gave it to him. By that time Steve had gone off to an urgent meeting. I didn't know what it was about at the time, but no doubt it was to seal the bargain with Garrity. It's quite a coup, you know, to have found a private backer in these days. Garrity may not be a genius, but you don't find many angels around like him.'

'You said Steve had personal problems, too, when we had lunch.'

'Did I? I shouldn't have done.'

'I think I may know what they are.'

'Then there's no need for me to say anything. As I say I shouldn't have mentioned it at lunch, but you're Steve's oldest friend, and I thought I should give you a hint about the way things are. I admire Steve very much, he's a wonderful person.' Again Dudley seemed to detect a note he did not care for, something almost subservient, in Race's voice.

The buffet in the dining room offered smoked salmon, glazed duck, all sorts of good things. He helped himself judiciously. Steve came up to him smiling.

'What have you been telling Garrity about me?'

'Nothing but good, I hope.'

'The story of the banger, what about that? He's talking

about my writing a history of the Anglo-American sausage.'

'And why not? I said it was an idea you and I had kicked around long ago, and Leslie was very much struck by it. He has flair, you know, or I wouldn't have taken him in.'

'Flair? Garrity?'

'Dudley, if you could see how you look.' He burst out laughing. 'It's a good job we're not serving bangers tonight.'

He stood in a corner of the dining room, gobbling glazed duck and hot chicken vol-au-vents in the uncomfortable manner enforced by stand-up buffets, and then was aware of somebody by his side. It was the housemaid. 'A telephone call for you, sir. You can take it in the hall.'

He put down his plate and followed her to the telephone, which stood in a small alcove beside a stand for sticks and umbrellas which was itself made in the shape of an umbrella. He knew, quite certainly, that this would be another call from Annabel Lee, and that when he picked up the little trimline instrument he would hear her light voice with its undertone of mockery. Would it be a recording, as he felt more and more sure the Yorkshire call had been? That seemed hardly possible, since she must have asked for him. The instrument looked harmless enough lying on its ledge, but he had to nerve himself to pick it up. He spoke his own name in a voice hardly above a whisper.

'He's gone,' were the words that entered his ear. The voice seemed unfamiliar. Was she playing some game?

'What do you mean? I don't understand you.'

'Dudley, it's Elaine. Your father. He's gone.' He could find nothing to say. 'Are you there?'

'Yes.' He took the instrument away from his ear, looked at it, put it back. 'Elaine, I'm sorry.'

'I told you he couldn't last more than a few days,' she said almost accusingly.

'Yes, you did. I hope seeing me didn't —'

'Nothing to do with it. The doctor said he might go at any time, and that's what happened. The doctor thinks he had another stroke. He died this afternoon.'

In the afternoon he had been at the zoo, assessing humans in animal terms. In adolescence he had believed his father to be a lion, but he had proved the most commonplace of monkeys. 'I thought you'd want to know.'

'Yes. Thank you very much. It's good of you to think of me at such a time.'

'After all, you're his son.' He did not comment. 'There's no need to come for the funeral. I said that too.'

'Elaine, I should have liked to come, but I really have to go back.'

'I said there was no need. And no need for excuses. We have plenty of friends up here. I wanted you to know, that's all.'

'Yes. Thank you.'

'All right, then.' He felt strongly that it was not all right, that there were words she expected him to say, some gesture that she wanted him to make. 'I don't suppose we'll talk to each other again. Goodbye, Dudley.'

He said goodbye, but the instrument at the other end had been put down before the word was out. Then he stood staring at the telephone as if it contained a secret that might be revealed by study. It struck him that in some way he could not understand his father's death was a decisive event, and that this severing of a tie he had thought broken long ago for some reason simplified his return to Graham. His father was dead, it seemed that he would never again see Annabel Lee, what was there to keep him? He picked up the instrument again, asked the operator for the transatlantic code, dialled Willie Rushmore's number. As he heard the ringing tone Bruxley passed him, no doubt in search of a lavatory, and awarded him a wave of the hand and a smile.

Then he heard Willie's voice, solemn and reliable. 'Professor Rushmore.'

'Willie, it's Dudley. I rang to ask if everything is all right.'

'I've covered up as well as I can, but all right, no, I can't say everything is *all right*. You should have written to Dexter. Or spoken to him.'

'I suppose so, yes. I wanted to get away. I thought if I saw Dexter he'd raise objections, read me a sermon.'

'I daresay he would have done. Rightly, in my opinion. Dexter was very hurt. There is a proper form for doing this kind of thing, if it has to be done. If a doctor or psychiatrist had seen you, said it was of real importance to your mental well-being, that you were under intolerable stress —'

'Yes, Willie, I know. I felt I didn't have time for all that. If the students are the trouble —'

'The students don't matter.' Willie coughed, and revised this slightly. 'I mean, I can handle the student question. But you'll have to explain ' to Dexter. In person, as you should have done before leaving.' Willie's voice grew warmer. 'If I had known you were going off in that harebrained way — well, it's done now, but you must come back.' There was a pause. 'Have you found her?'

'No.'

'I am not surprised. Nor sorry. She was no good to you, Dudley.'

'I saw my father while I was here. Now I've just learned that he has died. He was very ill.'

'I'm extremely sorry to hear that. But perhaps it may be a consolation that you saw him. Perhaps it gave a purpose to the whole visit.'

'You may be right. I'm coming back, Willie, I really am.'

'It sounds as though a party is going on.'

'Yes. The friend I'm staying with is giving one.'

'I see.'

'Please, Willie, I'm not here enjoying myself. I've been looking for Annabel Lee, and I've found out — I don't know exactly what, but something, something no good to me. But I'm coming back. I shall be on a flight tomorrow or Monday.'

'I'm delighted to hear it.' In a tone of conscious forbearance he added, 'I'll say no more, then.'

'And thank you for everything. I'm sorry I went off like that.'

'Not at all. We've been worried about you, Mary and I. I hope you've got it out of your system.' Willie waited for a comment on this, which he did not find it possible to make, then said in a faintly reproving tone, 'Mary sends her love,' and hung up.

He returned to the party, and found that it was spreading. The number of people seemed to have increased, and they were now in the dining and drawing rooms with a few young figures in jeans spilling over in the direction of the kitchen. He saw no sign of Phyl, but Steve waved to him across the room. He turned in the direction of the buffet, prepared to renew acquaintance with the glazed duck.

'My old friend Dudley, as I live and breathe,' a voice said, and he turned to find himself looking at the broad smiling features of George Garnish. The poet wore white trousers rather too tight for his bulk, a striped jacket reminiscent of the cricket blazers of Dudley's youth, and a large bright blue cravat. He had in tow a small pale delicately featured young man wearing a shirt that was frilled both at neck and cuffs, and a single long earring containing a large pearl. 'Dudley, this is Desmond, who thinks he's a poet but is more notable for other talents. Desmond, this is Dudley, last encountered in a Boston hotel room.'

Desmond said in a fluting voice, 'I'd never have thought it.'

'A wrong assumption, Desmond. And those who make wrong assumptions will be punished for their errors.'

'Really, Garnish, you are *tiresome* sometimes.' Desmond shrugged an elegant shoulder.

'Dudley will know what I mean.'

He shook his head, in part to show that he did not know what Garnish was talking about, but also because he felt a numbness, an absence of emotion that carried within it the seed of pain. *I forgive you*, he had said to the dying figure on the bed who had once been handsome Dr Donald Potter. He had forgiven the man who said, "Watch out, here's a tweaky one" when bowling to him in the garden. What did he feel about that? Like a dental patient anaesthetised, nothing at all.

'What's that?' Garnish asked.

'What do you mean?'

'I was saying you were looking for Annabel Lee in that Boston hotel, and you said "Nothing at all".'

'Did I? I was thinking of something else.'

'I don't know what you're talking about,' Desmond said. 'Poe wrote about Annabel Lee, didn't he? Such a boring poem, it goes up and down like a seesaw.'

'It was a real woman named Annabel Lee that Dudley

was looking for. Still is, I expect. Eh?' The numbness wrapped Dudley like a blanket. 'I don't suppose you've found her. The inaccessible she, right? Where'er she be, that inaccessible she, who doth control my heart and me — isn't that how you feel?' In the poet's big brown bloodshot eyes there was amusement, good humour, and something else. A gleam of malice?

'Perhaps.'

'Edgar's the clue.'

'I've had enough of this, Garnish, I'll leave you with your *friend*.' Desmond turned his back on them, slithered away through the crowd.

'Little devil,' Garnish said affectionately. 'You wouldn't believe what he's like in bed. Edgar's the clue, the secret, the worm in the bud. What was in the purloined letter, what did the tell-tale heart say, what made the House of Usher fall into the tarn? That's where to look.'

'Where?'

The other seemed to have forgotten the question. 'I'm just back from that States trip, a good trip, a real whirl. That's what life should be, agreed?'

'What?'

'Why, whirling. Drop an Elmer here, pick up a Desmond there. But that's not Potter's way, is it? Potter's fixed on Annabel Lee. Know where to find her?'

He maintained his monosyllables with another, 'Where?'

'In the House of Usher, where else?'

If Garrity was not in his right mind, perhaps Garnish was simply high. Or was it his own sensation of numbness that made him feel the other was talking, not precisely nonsense but an unknown language in need of interpretation? When he spoke he felt words forming in his mouth, and emerging with the difficulty he had known after dental anaesthesia.

'Where is it, then? Where is the House of Usher?'

'There is one in every big city, but this is New York's House of Usher. It has no name, it has no number, it is simply the House of Usher that once fell but has now risen again. It is the heart of the maelstrom, the centre of the whirlpool. It is what my poems are about, what civilisation means. The House of Usher rises from the ruins, it fell because of the decay of a civilisation, it rises again and is that decay.'

Garnish uttered these mysterious phrases eloquently, fluently, even with passion. A part of Dudley's mind marked this and thought there was no surprise about the poet's success with students, even while his anaesthetised mouth said, 'You'll have to explain. I don't understand you.'

The other looked frowningly at his large plump hands, as though expecting them to show visible signs of the decay he had been talking about. Then he spoke, with anger and apparent dislike. The powerful fumes of gin came from his mouth.

'That's right, you don't understand. You don't understand and you don't like. Don't like queers in striped jackets writing poems about animals getting back at humans, you think we're just getting back at society, isn't that so? Don't like queers with pearl earrings, don't like men going to bed with each other, don't like me talking about it.'

'I've got no feelings about it either way.'

'Come on now, maybe you can kid yourself but you can't kid GG, I saw the way you looked in that hotel room, the way you looked at little Des. Well.' He stopped, brooding for a moment, and Dudley was about to move away when the poet's hand dropped on his shoulder. 'You don't like, you don't understand and you don't *know*.' A hand pulled power-fully at his arm. 'Come here, c'mon over here.' He let himself be led to the window. 'Look out, just look and tell me what you see.'

He looked out. Beyond the front garden lay the quiet St John's Wood road. A woman was taking her spaniel for an evening constitutional, the dog firmly on a leash. On the street corner two old fellows gossiped beneath a street lamp. A second lamp, up the road, sent a ghostly light through the lime trees on to the pavements.

'Well,' Garnish asked. '*Well?*'

'A peaceful road in a prosperous part of London, looking much the same as it has for the past twenty years.' As he spoke these words he became aware of some presence behind his right shoulder. How long had it been there? He did not turn to see what it was.

'Wrong. It may look the same, but it isn't. That's a vulgar error, a vulgar bourgeois error. One day, tonight, tomorrow, next week, that woman's going to be mugged, lucky if she gets away with a few lost teeth. Those old fools up there, one of them lives down a mews, he'll have his skull split open soon as he turns off the road. They'll get the other as he puts the key in his door, force a way in, smash up the place looking for his money, leave him tied up and gagged, lucky if the police find him in time.'

'Things like that don't happen in St John's Wood.'

'They will. Believe me, Mr Prissy Pants, they will. That's what my poems are about. You know what I tell those boys and girls who ask questions? I tell them the future belongs to inhumanity. Those science fiction films, they're rubbish but they've got something. The future doesn't belong to human beings, it belongs to monsters. You don't see it, though. Lucky you.' The look of anger, malice, contempt, faded from Garnish's eye, which remained merely bloodshot. 'Here endeth the first and last lesson. I like you, Dudley, but I tell you what it is. You don't know what life's all about.'

With a parting tap on the shoulder, a tap that was almost a punch, he moved away. Now Dudley turned to see, moving away also, the neat figure of Paul Race. This, then, was the presence he had felt behind him. Race smiled feebly, but did not speak. His face was of a ghastly pallor. He must have been listening to the conversation, but what could there have been in Garnish's drunken vision of apocalypse that so disturbed him?

Apocalypse, he thought as he wandered through rooms filled with faces that seemed suddenly to have become those of animals and birds of prey, so that he saw a hyena's snarl in an old man's laugh, head thrown back to reveal yellow fangs. In another gaze bent on a woman he saw the cold assessment of a vulture waiting to descend, in the smile of a bare-backed girl the provocation of the bitch wishing to be trampled. He had drunk little, yet now felt that delusive clarity, that dissociation of the senses from the actual, he had sometimes experienced near the end of a drinking session.

154

He could not have said afterwards how long he had spent leaning against a wall in the dining room, deterring the few people who spoke to him with monosyllabic replies, watching the guests stuffing food into their mouths with animal eagerness, seeing the supercilious looks cast occasionally by the waiters, or keepers, upon their charges. There was a moment when he became aware that people were leaving, another when he felt his hand grasped and saw that it was in the grip of little Leslie, Sir Leslie Garrity, Bart, who was expressing pleasure at meeting him. Moments or minutes later there was Steve, beaming and asking if he had enjoyed the party. He said that he had.

'I saw you talking to George Garnish. Didn't know you'd met him.'

'He came and read some of his work at Graham.'

'Great poet. Influential too. I'd like to get him on the Otter list. Dudley, are you all right? You look a little wan.'

'I had some bad news.' He told Steve about Elaine's call.

'I'm very sorry. But it's not as if you'd been close. You must be pleased that you saw him before the end.'

'He asked my forgiveness. And I gave it. Don't you think there's something terrible about that, a son forgiving his father?'

'Let's face it, you had something to forgive.'

'Steve, what did Garnish mean talking about the House of Usher? He said I should look for Annabel Lee in the House of Usher, that fell once but had risen again. Was it all nonsense, do you think?'

'I only know the Poe story. The House of Usher was rotten, had a crack in it, and eventually collapsed into the waters of the tarn. Is that what you mean?'

'I don't know. I'm repeating what Garnish said. I hoped you might understand it.'

' 'Fraid not, old man. Never am quite sure what George is getting at, but he's a fine writer. Blood and guts.' Steve clenched his fist and laughed. 'Rosemary, love, what is it?'

'Daddy, I want to show you something.'

'Show me what? What do you mean? It'll wait.'

'No, it won't. Come on, Daddy.'

She took his hand, and Steve's face crumpled. The

vigorous, aggressive features seemed to blur as though a waxen image was dissolving under heat, so that what had been distinct, hard and powerful was now softly uncertain.

'No,' he said. 'No, Rosemary.'

'You then,' she said to Dudley. He felt her hand gripping his own. 'You're not afraid.'

'Please, Rosemary. You mustn't.' Steve covered his face with his hands.

She looked at him with a blank face, pushed Dudley towards the stairs. They went up the curving elegant staircase. At the top she put a finger to her lips and led him to the right, away from his own room. She stopped at a closed door, her fingers white, gripping the gold door handle. Then she flung open the door, shouting '*Voilà.*'

He had never seen Steve and Phyl's bedroom, and its appearance came as a shock. There were curtains in a delicate shade of pink, a large shell-shaped bed with an elaborately carved headboard, a thick oyster-coloured carpet. Around the walls were panels after Watteau and Fragonard showing nymphs and shepherds sporting amorously in sylvan scenes. A ceiling picture showed Daphnis and Chloe, with Daphnis holding out a hand to touch the maiden's breast. The whole was illuminated by lighting that went around all four walls and looked, he might have thought or even said on another occasion, like a tart's attempt at rococo taste. At present, however, his attention was drawn to the central feature of the tableau, which revealed Phyl and Bill Bruxley naked on the bed, engaged in what was undoubtedly sexual activity.

Phyl moved off Bruxley and said, 'Oh, hell.'

'You see. I told you they were screwing,' Rosemary said triumphantly.

Phyl got off the bed, snatched up her pink housecoat and put it on. 'Darling, I've said before that I do *not* wish you to use that word. And Dud, what *can* you be thinking of to come bursting into my bedroom.'

He had time to think admiringly that if you found yourself at the centre of such a scene, this undoubtedly was the way in which to carry it off, before he was pushed violently aside. Steve moved past him into the room. In his right hand he held a carving knife, perhaps the one used to cut the ham or slice the duck. Muttering unintelligibly he advanced in the direction of Bruxley, who scrambled off the bed and retreated towards the wall, snatching up a pair of shorts on the way.

Rosemary put her hand to her mouth and gasped. Phyl, as it seemed given confidence by the housecoat, said, 'Steve, give me that knife. You're making yourself look ridiculous.'

Steve ignored her, and continued to approach Bruxley. The doctor, in a late gesture towards modesty, had one leg in his shorts. When Steve made a slash at him, however, he lost balance and fell to the floor. Steve bent over him menacingly, making weaving gestures with the knife. Bruxley, at his feet, put his arms round Steve's legs, whether to bring him down or to ask for mercy was not clear.

Phyl screamed.

Like a man in a slow motion film, Steve sank to the ground, still waving the carving knife. Some sort of action seemed necessary and Dudley moved forward, aware of Phyl's frightened face and of Rosemary also looking at the bodies on the floor, hand placed to mouth as if to stifle any sound she might be weak enough to utter. Dudley's own actions were not of lightning speed, since he felt the difficulty of separating the two men to resemble that of parting two fighting dogs. As if to justify this simile, the begging Bruxley changed his tactics, or perhaps was merely trying to escape from his attacker. In any case he made vigorous pumping gestures with both legs, rather as though enacting *Knees up Mother Brown* on the floor. One knee caught Steve in the groin, the other leg entangled itself in Dudley's, so that he was brought down on top of them both, like a man piling into a rugby scrum.

Whether because of this impact or the knee in the groin, Steve let out a loud groan and rolled off Bruxley, who scrambled up and put on his trousers, his handsome face contorted with anger. Phrases were ejected from his mouth in bursts.

'Disgusting scene — psycho-social behaviour — violent

attack — reasonable discussion —'

Steve lay, or partly crouched, on the floor holding his genitals. 'What is there to discuss? You were screwing my wife.'

Bruxley found his tie, put it on. He said severely, 'Civilised people talk these things out reasonably. You have a marital problem, Steve —'

Steve snorted. Dudley got up. Phyl screamed again. Rosemary took her hand from her mouth, pointed at Dudley and said, 'Look.'

Dudley glanced down. Drops of liquid were running from his left hand to the carpet. He saw with surprise that the liquid was red.

At that the whole scene changed again, the slow motion film speeded up. Phyl rushed out, mouthing the word *bandages*, Steve got up from the floor and put down the red-stained carving knife with extreme care as if it were a piece of evidence in a criminal case, Bruxley helped Dudley to take off his jacket. In his collapse on to the struggling bodies, Dudley had evidently almost impaled himself on the carving knife, which had made a tear in jacket and shirt and inflicted a wound just below the shoulder. Steve was profusely apologetic.

'Dudley, what an awful thing to happen.'

'It shows that you should never get mixed up in somebody else's argument.'

'Coming in here with a carving knife, I don't know what I was thinking of.'

'It's not an unusual reaction,' Bruxley observed and then checked himself, feeling perhaps that the comment was out of place.

Phyl came back with iodine, plasters and bandages, and called Rosemary to come and help. In five minutes he was patched up. When Phyl asked whether it hurt, he answered truthfully that he hardly felt it. She looked at the jacket.

'It's ruined.' Certainly there was a jagged tear, as well as the bloodstains.

'Order another on Monday. Charge it to me.' That was Steve.

'Thanks. But I shall fly back tomorrow if I can get a seat

on a plane.'

'Oh my God, I've driven you away.'

'Nothing to do with this evening, it's just that —' Just what? He hardly knew, and let the sentence fade away. He was aware of a need to sit down, and a reluctance to do so in this bedroom. 'I should like to go somewhere else.'

'Darling, of *course*,' Phyl said. 'Steve, take Dud downstairs and give him a brandy. He's had an awful shock. Bill, you'd better go home.' Bruxley nodded gravely, like one physician approving another's diagnosis.

'Is that all, then?' Rosemary, standing at the door, asked incredulously. Phyl, now fully in command, turned on her daughter.

'You're a little mischief maker, Rosemary. If it weren't for you, none of this would have happened. Dud wouldn't have hurt his arm.'

The girl appealed to her father. 'Daddy, aren't you going to *do* something about it?'

Steve shrugged.

'Your father and I will talk about the whole situation, but not now.' Bruxley began to say something, but Phyl cut him short. 'For heaven's sake, Bill, do as I said and go home. Steve, take Dud downstairs. I want a few words with Rosemary.'

Rosemary's face was contorted with fury. She rubbed away tears from her eyes. 'I *don't* want to talk to you, you randy old bitch,' she cried, and ran out of the room. They heard a door close, a key turn.

'I'll talk to her, you go down.'

They obeyed her instructions. In the hall, Bruxley gave them an uneasy good night, and went out. Steve and Dudley went into the dining room. Relics of the party were around everywhere, empty and part-filled glasses, bits of food on plates, ashtrays crammed with butts. Steve looked round gloomily.

'Smiling Service, that's the people we hired, only serve, they don't clear up. I'll see if I can find a clean glass.' He returned with glasses of brandy, handed one to Dudley, drank most of his own at a gulp. 'Now you know the family secret. Phyl and I don't sleep together, haven't done for a couple of years.'

'You knew about Bruxley?'

'Of course. He's not the first. Can't explain it really, I can still get it up, you know. It's just — you go off each other. Mutual, I suppose you might call it.'

'Steve. Did you have an affair with Annabel Lee? Was that part of the trouble?'

Steve looked at him with what seemed genuine astonishment. 'Whatever put that idea into your head?'

'Did you?'

'Of course not. Mind you, she was attractive in an odd way — you know that better than me. But I simply took her out to lunch as I told you, then asked her to that dinner, which was a bit of a disaster though nothing like as bad as Phyl makes out. But nothing else, nothing at all. I never made a pass, feel sure she'd have turned me down if I had. It's simply, as I say, you go off each other.'

'So why not get divorced? Or at least separate?'

'Good question, don't know that I can answer it. Suits me to have a wife, someone to act as hostess at dinner parties, look after guests. Phyl does it very well, people like her, I think she enjoys it. As for the rest, no need to worry about me.'

'How do you mean?'

'I have a quarter of a share in a girl —'

'A *quarter* of a *share*?'

'Quite a usual arrangement,' Steve said, with a touch of impatience. 'We've put her in a flat, pay her a monthly salary, then she's available to each of us on so many days a month.'

'Who else has a share? Paul Race?'

'Lord no, what made you think that? The others are all managing directors or chairmen of firms we deal with. Works very well. But of course I wouldn't want to install a girl like that here. And as I say, Phyl likes playing hostess, and we get on pretty well for the most part, I don't think she'd want to move out. Suits me as well.' He thought of Steve's look of misery in the bedroom, but said nothing. 'Trouble is, she can be a bit blatant sometimes.'

'What an extraordinary way to go on. I never heard anything like it.'

'Doesn't happen at Graham? I bet it does, old man, I bet it does. I'm sorry it should have spoiled your party, though, and truly sorry as hell about your arm. Not much of a party, where the guest ends up stabbed by the host.' He hooted with laughter. 'Here's Phyl now. How is she?'

'All right, I think. That girl, though, she really does enjoy making mischief. Darling, I'd like a drink too, even though I have had one or two this evening.' She was still wearing the pink house coat. 'What a *shambles*.' It was impossible to know whether she referred to the bedroom scene or the condition of the drawing room. 'Darling Dud, I'm so sorry. Do *please* stay, or we'll feel we've driven you away, the two of us.'

He wanted to tell them that his father's death was an occasion of immense significance, that in some way it severed his last links with England, but the words would not come. Instead he said, 'Bleek tells me they believe Wolfdale was killed because of some trouble with one of the bosses in the drug ring he was part of, personal trouble. Anyway, that's the official line. And after that phone call in Yorkshire it seems useless to look for Annabel Lee any longer. So I may as well go back. One thing, though, Phyl, a question I've asked Steve already and drawn a blank, but I'll ask you. What do you know about the House of Usher? I know it's a story by Poe, but what else? Does it mean anything to you apart from that?'

'Darling, how fascinating. I'm afraid I don't know anything, but is it a kind of *clue*? Who told you about it?'

'George Garnish, the poet.'

'*That* one. I wouldn't take anything he said too seriously.' She hesitated, went on. 'Talking of seriousness, I'm sorry, Steve too, I'm sure, about what you saw upstairs. It doesn't mean much, you know. Steve and I have a relationship, we understand each other.'

'So he was telling me.'

'We are living in the eighties, after all. A relationship has to be modern, like everything else.'

'I hope Rosemary understands that.'

'Of course she does, you old prune. Honestly, Dud, that's

what you are, simply an old *prune*.'

'Garnish called me Prissy Pants.'

'That just wasn't polite. But Rosemary knows perfectly well what goes on, she just likes to make trouble. There's no need to talk about such things, or to use coarse language as she does.'

'Perhaps if the things didn't happen —'

'I'm not going to argue about it. Nor is Steve, are you, darling?' Steve shook his head. 'I'm tired and I'm going to bed, and darling Dud, I hope you have a good night's sleep and that your arm doesn't hurt too much.'

It was a long time before he fell asleep. He lived over again those minutes in the strange house when the telephone had rung and he had heard Annabel Lee's voice. He tried to reconstruct the conversation as one may retrace in memory the lines of a loved face, and above all to decide whether the click with which the connection was broken had come from the replacement of the instrument on its cradle or whether it was the end of a recording. In the house, sitting on the bed, the papier mâché bust of Poe beside him, he had thought it was a recording, but perhaps the click had existed only in his imagination. I must go tomorrow, he thought, and resolved that the first thing he would do in the morning would be to make a flight reservation. He would do it himself, because he felt that Steve and Phyl might somehow stop him, so that he could remain with them as permanent witness to their modern relationship. *Flight* — the word was appropriate.

His sleep was visited by nightmares. In one Rosemary pursued him, knife in hand, saying: 'I am the cloud by night, chilling and killing your Annabel Lee.' Then she plunged the knife into her own breast. Slowly as treacle, blood oozed out.

Yet in the morning these night thoughts and nightmares seemed absurd. The party debris had gone, cleared up presumably by the resident maid. Phyl, wearing another housecoat that matched in colour the dark and light blue stripes of the dining room wallpaper, poured coffee, offered toast and four different jams and marmalades, her smile wide and welcoming. Steve had nicked himself shaving, but was otherwise genial as usual. When Dudley mentioned making a flight reservation Steve, far from putting any obstacle in his way, offered to do it for him. Phyl laid a hand on his wrist.

'Darling, you're not leaving because of us, are you? To spare us *embarrassment*? Because you shouldn't.'

'It isn't that. I have to 'get back, this is the middle of a semester. Perhaps I shouldn't have come.'

'Poor dear old Dud, what it is to be in love.'

'Isn't that what you are?'

'Oh, come *on* now. You don't seriously think that fandango last night had anything to do with love.' Into his mind came a vision of Annabel Lee talking about separating action from feeling, and saying, "Action is pure, feeling is just slop". But Phyl was speaking. 'Wasn't it Aldous Huxley who said love wouldn't exist if the word hadn't been invented? Something like that.'

'I don't know whether it was Huxley, but it sounds to me pretty fair nonsense.'

'Dud, you're so romantic. Don't blush, it's a nice thing to be, I envy you. I'm sorry you haven't found the lady, though as I said when I first heard about her, I think you're lucky. What you need is a nice girl, one of your students perhaps.'

'To them I'm an old man.'

Rosemary appeared at the door. 'Mum, I'm just off to see Geraldine. 'Lo, Dud.'

'You've had no breakfast.'

'Don't want any. At Geraldine's they have doughnuts.'

'And Mr Potter's probably leaving today, you may not see him again.'

'Oh well, goodbye then. Next time perhaps you'll have a proper American accent. And a different name.'

'Perhaps. Goodbye, Rosemary.'

'That girl is a *trial*,' Phyl said again when they heard the front door close. 'Doughnuts, indeed. She'll be smoking pot with Geraldine all the morning, then come back starry-eyed saying she doesn't want lunch. How's your shoulder?'

'Not bad. Aches a bit.'

'Make sure a doctor looks at it when you get back. Here's Steve. Any luck? Not that I consider it lucky to lose you, darling Dud.' Steve said he had got Dudley a flight late that afternoon, Phyl made a face to show that she was sorry, and went off to her bath. Steve rubbed his hands.

'Glad Phyl's gone. I wanted a private word.' He buttered himself a piece of toast. What was coming now? After that quarter-share in a girl, what further admission of modern living was Steve about to make? However vivid the end of the previous night was in his memory, it seemed to have been eliminated from that of his host. Steve ate some toast and marmalade, then said, 'Have you thought any further about it?'

'About what?'

'The history of the banger. Leslie mentioned it to you last night.'

'You can't be serious.'

'Never more so. It's got a terrific potential, don't you see? You do the American end, I do the English. And we make it nationwide, that's the trick.' He held up a hand to forestall objections. 'I'm not suggesting you tour every State in person, of course not. You employ tasters, people we can call food experts, out-of-work hotel chefs who don't mind making a few dollars on the side, you know the kind of thing. How do the Eastern and Western states compare? Isn't there something called Philadelphia scrapple, haven't I heard of country sausage? What about the deep South, they must have new ingredients, different blending. What kind of sausages do cowboys eat? Same over here. Did you know there's a special Indian sausage, curry-flavoured? And others with cheese and herbs, no meat at all? That's only the beginning. All right, I can understand a book like this is too low grade for you to want to give a lot of time to it, but how about acting as general editor, co-ordinating contributions, something like that? There'd be money in it.'

There'd be money in it: the words still rang in his ears as the plane rose from the ground at Heathrow.

PART THREE

1 *The Wisdom of Abel Blumfeld*

They should have touched down in early evening, but the plane dawdled about the sky, as it seemed endlessly and in fact for nearly two hours. They were told of congestion at Kennedy. Head back, eyes closed, Dudley thought about the people he had seen, the things said to him, then tried quite consciously to make his mind blank. This was a way of clearing the mind that had been strongly recommended to him by Dilip something-or-other, an elegant Indian who taught courses in Eastern religion and philosophy at Graham. When confronted by a knotty practical or emotional problem, Dilip said, you should clear out the ordinary paraphernalia cluttering the mind, throw it all out as on to a rubbish dump so that the unencumbered mind might float, ready for ideas to enter. I try to do this, he thought, and what is the result? I forget Dilip's surname.

Then he remembered the name, which was the common one of Singh, and at the same moment the thought entered his mind: *what caused the fire in El Paso?* He had asked this question mentally more than once, but had then pushed it aside in favour of other things. Now it floated back, and seemed of prime importance. Had the fire been purely accidental? Was it not remarkable that Lenore should die in December, and that within three months Annabel Lee should disappear? What later stories about the fire and its causes had appeared in — what was it? The *El Paso Daily Journal*. As the plane circled meaninglessly in the sky, it seemed that the Dilip Singh approach had provided a key that might unlock the door leading to the truth.

To see the paper he would need access to a newspaper library or morgue, and it seemed vitally important that this should be done as soon as possible. When at last they touched down at Kennedy he rang Rod Sterling, a reporter he knew on the *New York Times*, to learn that he was away for the weekend and would not be in the office until midday on Monday. He called Willie, said that he would be back on Monday, and booked into a hotel.

At seven-thirty he was in Donohue's, a bar in the Thirties on Lexington, drinking Scotch and trying to achieve again that state in which his mind floated, unencumbered. He sat on a bar stool looking first at the names on the bottles in front of him, then into the Scotch which, even in the bar's American darkness, had a golden glow. If one looked into that amber liquid, absenting oneself completely from the past and the future, from New York and London, what might be revealed?

'Professor. Professor Potter.'

His question was answered, here was the revelation, a tall young man in a blue suit, a figure quite unknown.

The young man took the next stool. 'You don't remember me?'

'I'm afraid not.'

'Blumfeld, Abel Blumfeld. Ten years back. I took your course on the English novel, another on Poe and Whitman.'

Blumfeld, Blumfeld? Yes, with the name the face emerged clearly enough, a gangling student from Brooklyn, so thin that if he stood sideways you'd hardly see him as the old saying went, big Jewish nose, horn-rimmed spectacles done up with tape, black hair that stood up on end, always untidy, a glutton for work, bright ideas but too full of himself, editor of the student newspaper. That was Blumfeld.

A memory came to him. 'You were the one who set *me* a paper. On Whitman, wasn't it?'

Ten years ago he had still been green enough to be rattled when he made mistakes, and one day in talking about Whitman he had got a quotation wrong, misdated another poem, given a wrong title to a third. Blumfeld had picked him up on all of them, and a couple of days later had come in with what he called a Test Paper for the Professor, consisting of ten questions relating to Whitman's background, activities, poetry, all with factual answers. Blumfeld's manner when handing it in — he had made copies which he distributed round the class — was a mixture of cockiness at showing he knew so much, and a sort of shamefaced hope that the Professor would get angry and tear up the paper.

Fortunately he had done nothing of the kind, but had answered all ten questions off the cuff, so that when he had finished the rest of the class burst into spontaneous applause. It was Blumfeld who shifted uneasily, pretended to laugh, and said that of course if he'd set a really tough set of questions — but at that he was shouted down. When that happened he had stood there glaring round at them all, his large hands twisting together. To be the brightest student in class hadn't been enough for Blumfeld, he wanted also to be brighter than the man teaching him. Perhaps he had been, but he had gone the wrong way to demonstrate it.

Now, however, Blumfeld showed no embarrassment. 'Right, right. And you knew all the answers.' To the bartender he said, 'Gimme the usual.'

'Coming up.'

But could this really be Blumfeld? It was not just that the gangling young boy had filled out into a leanly elegant figure, that the untidy hair was smoothly polished and neatly parted, the taped-up hornrims replaced by rimless spectacles, and the jeans and patched pullover by a suit of evident quality. All that might be attributed to the natural workings of time and prosperity. But in some way Blumfeld seemed to be a different person. Had he had his nose straightened, or was it just that his face had filled out? There was a kind of sleekness about him utterly unlike the Blumfeld Dudley had known. A dissatisfied mongrel had turned into a contented cat, perhaps that was the transformation.

The bartender placed not one, but three Martinis in front of Blumfeld. He nodded, picked one up, downed it at a gulp, sighed with contentment.

'So how's everything back at the thought factory? Still turning out highly civilised kids, ready to take their places among the nation's top earners?' On his wide mouth there was the half-smile of an adult enquiring about the amusements of children.

'We do our best. You look as if you might have taken a place there yourself.'

'I don't complain. Never seen you in Donohue's before.'

'I'm just passing through. I've been in England for a few days, going back to Graham tomorrow.'

Blumfeld merely nodded. Evidently an academic who jetted across the Atlantic for a few days in the middle of a semester was something he took in his stride. 'I often think of you, know that? Not you so much as Graham, a liberal arts education, all that crap.'

'Is it crap?'

'Sure it is, when you get down to it. Say you're an attorney, how does the old beauty and truth routine help with plea bargaining? How far does Proust get you if you're into computers? And old Walt, I used to be strong on Walt, he ain't much use if you're vice president of an insurance company.'

'Is that what you are?'

'Nah. Managing editor at Stevens-Pangbourne.'

Dudley knew the name vaguely, as that of a conglomerate that published dozens of different magazines, most of them professional or technical. 'So perhaps a liberal arts education was some use after all.'

Blumfeld's mouth opened, showing a range of what were no doubt capped teeth, but no sound emerged. At the end of this bout of silent laughter he wiped his eyes with a silk handkerchief with the intials "AB" marked in one corner, and said: 'Perhaps. You married?'

'No. Are you?'

'Was. Twice. Got unhitched again a few months back.' He drank half of the second Martini. 'Not for me. No, sir, marriage is not for me.'

A thought occurred to Dudley. 'Do you have a library or a morgue at Stevens-Pangbourne?'

'The whole place is a morgue, some say.' The silent laugh briefly rocked him again. 'Agree with them on a bad day. Whaddya want?'

'Would it contain out-of-town papers?'

'Sure, sure. You want another of those?'

He said yes, and pursued the point. 'One published in El Paso?'

'I guess so, why not? Probably find we own a few mags out in Texas, got to keep in touch. What's your interest?'

'Do you think it would be possible to get access to the library? I want to look up some details in an El Paso paper, details covering the last three months or maybe a little more. The *El Paso Daily Journal.*'

'Look 'em up then, why not?'

'I mean tonight?'

'No problem. For Abel Blumfeld keys turn, doors open, anything is possible. Mind, I don't guarantee we've got the paper, but if we do you can see it. Only one thing. Before we go I need another drink.'

'Of course.'

But it was another row of three Martinis that were placed in front of Blumfeld. He finished the last of the earlier batch and started on the second round. 'When I say line 'em up Joe here lines 'em up. Ain't that right, Joe?' Joe said it was right. 'Don't suppose you've seen Martinis drunk this way before.'

'No, I haven't. But when Edmund Wilson was in his seventies he'd go into the Princeton Club, have six Martinis in front of him at once and drink his way through them, talking all the time about books, ideas and people.'

'Edmund Wilson, eh. Good company.' Blumfeld looked down at his drink. 'I wrote a novel once, know that? And got it published.'

'About the problems of a Jewish boy struggling to make it in New York?'

'Yeah, more or less. That and my first marriage. How d'you know?'

He already regretted the remark. 'It's the kind of thing most first novels are about.'

'Is that so, is that so? *Times* said it was promising. Sold two thousand copies. Very smart you are, Professor. What do you pull back a year?' In the face of this aggressiveness Dudley regretted the remark still more. It seemed wise to answer. Blumfeld sneered. 'I make more'n twice that. Maybe you're not so smart.'

'I never said I was. Did you write another novel?'

'What would have been the point? Matter of fact I did, it was turned down. See what I mean, though, about liberal arts being crap? All that stuff about great poets, great novelists, Melville, Hawthorne, Poe, Whitman. I used to think it meant something, but what does it do? Does it put money in the bank for anybody? Except you, of course, it gives you a living, you and the rest of the faculty, all the faculties all over America. Not too much of a living, but you might say it keeps you in employment. The writers themselves, though, what do they get? Ninety-nine out of a hundred don't have a pot to piss in. And they ain't the worst, mind, it's the worst who ring the cash register.'

'Not always. I believe Saul Bellow makes a healthy income.'

'Saul Bellow.' Blumfeld looked into his drink, shook his head and muttered something inaudible but evidently uncomplimentary, perhaps about Saul Bellow, perhaps about

171

liberal arts professors, perhaps even about Dudley himself. It might be best to move away from the question of Blumfeld's writings, before he decided to cancel that visit to the library. The roll call of writers struck a chord in Dudley's mind. He said, 'The House of Usher.'

'What about it? Story by Poe. I wrote you an essay, "Psychic Interpretations of Poe's *House of Usher*", remember that?'

'I can't say I do.'

'You said it was the most interesting view of the story you'd ever had from a student.' Behind the rimless glasses Blumfeld's gaze was less hostile than hurt.

'I'm sorry, I'd forgotten. I didn't mean Poe's story. I meant—' He remembered Garnish's words, and repeated them as nearly as he could. 'Every big city has one, but I mean New York's House of Usher. It has no name or number, it's simply New York's House of Usher. Do you know what I mean?'

Blumfeld took off his spectacles and stared at him. With the protective glass removed his eyes could be seen to protrude, the eyeballs seeming to bulge from their sockets. He went into the soundless laughter routine, but this time almost in a paroxysm, rocking back and forth till he looked likely to fall off the stool. He finished another Martini, so that there was only one to go. Then he wiped his eyes and replaced the glasses. Dudley watched in bewilderment.

'Professor Potter, you of all people. If I'd been told this by somebody else I wouldn'ta believed it.'

'I don't understand. You know what I'm talking about?'

'That's what a liberal arts educator wants to know, where's the House of Usher.'

He said desperately, 'Look here. I don't have a personal interest. A poet in London told me — I'm looking for somebody and I was told I might find them here, in the House of Usher.' This set Blumfeld off again. Dudley waited until he had finished. 'I don't understand the joke, but if you can tell me where to find the House of Usher I'll be grateful.'

Blumfeld, still shaking with inner merriment, plunged an arm down from his stool and plucked up from the bar's darkness, as if from the sea bed, one of those document cases that are necessary equipment for a modern executive. He took out of it a magazine. The cover showed a young man and woman, both naked, clinched in an embrace that made it difficult to tell exactly what kind of sexual activity occupied them. Above them was the magazine's title: *Shacking Up*. Blumfeld leafed through the pages until he found the advertisement he was looking for. It was a half-page, illustrated by a Gothic building full of spires and slit windows, with tiny figures entering its half-open door. Around the advertisement, serving as a border, was a coiled whip. The text said only: *The House of Usher*, with a telephone number below it.

'What is this? There's no address.'

'Right. Just like you said, no address. It changes each time. You call this number, get a recorded message that tells you where the House of Usher is next — it's open two or three times a week — how much it'll cost you to get in. That'll be anything from fifty to a hundred dollars, according to what goes.'

'But what is it? What are you paying money for?'

'An S-M show. You know what S-M is, Professor?'

'Sado-masochism, yes.'

'Right again. The House of Usher gives you the best S-M show in Manhattan. There are others, but this is the best. Though mind you, it's still a kinda tourist trap. That number and no address gag gives visitors a kick, they think they're doing something they shouldn't. Maybe so, but it's not illegal, nothing to stop you doing what you want if you're over eighteen, whether you're white, black or yellow. Ask me, how do I know? Answer is it's part of the job.'

He riffled through *Shacking Up* until he came to the contents page. Beside titles like *Hong Kong, Sophisticated Sin City* and *Clarissa's Comeuppance* was a panel containing the names of editorial staff. At the top was Abel Blumfeld, Managing Editor.

'Come on then, say it. Is this the best Graham could do for a nice bright Jewish boy? What makes you run a mag like this, Abel, your thoughts should be on higher things. I'll tell you why, shall I? Because I do it well, because I like it, because it's no worse than any other crap, because it pays off in four hundred dollar suits and an East Side apartment. That, Professor, is the wisdom of Abel Blumfeld.'

'You said you worked for Stevens-Pangbourne.'

'So I do. Did you think Stevens-Pangbourne just ran mags about how to make your own china cabinets and what goes on inside the guts of cars? You know what old man Gaylord Stevens said to me one day? "I've got a standard reply when people ask what business I'm in. The business of making money, is what I tell 'em. If you're making money for me, Abel, I'll make money for you, just remember that. If you don't, what use are you?" I haven't forgotten it.' Blumfeld drained his last Martini and said, with something of the savagery he had shown when talking about his own novels, 'We're a subsidiary, mind, along with a dozen others, Hotnumbeı Mags. But I don't let it worry me if old Gaylord's a snob, an I-know-the-Kennedys snob, a Great Society snob, a send-my-kids-to-the-best-private-schools snob, a liberal arts education crap snob. I know it's all about making money. Should I let it worry me, Professor?'

He thought of the library, and refrained from comment.

'You don't like to say anything in case I change my mind about taking you along to look for that Texas paper, am I right?' His grip on Dudley's arm was painfully tight. 'Never fear, Abel Blumfeld remains the nice Jewish boy you remember, he'd do anything for his old Prof, and not a word will he breathe to anyone about the House of Usher.'

'I told you I was looking for somebody.'

'You did, and I believe you. But what will you do when you find them?' Hand still gripping arm, but good humour restored, Blumfeld led him out of Donohue's darkness into the neon brightness of the New York night. In the taxi his grip relaxed, he leaned back, patted Dudley's arm.

'You can rely on Abel Blumfeld. He never let anyone down. This paper, no need to worry, if it's there you'll see it. With me looking after you there'll be no trouble.' He began to hum some unrecognisable tune. 'Just back from England, you say? How was it?'

'Too much like America.'

'Is that so? I'll tell you something. You think, people think, Abel's a New Yorker, must love Manhattan. Not true, Professor, I hate it. Hated it for years. But I'll tell you something else, any other city I'd hate worse.'

The Stevens-Pangbourne building was on Sixth Avenue, a rectangular slab shooting up into the sky. Blumfeld's steps wavered slightly as they approached the darkened entrance, and Dudley's heart sank, but within the building all went as smoothly as he had said. He was evidently known and respected, and the night manager made no demur when he asked for the keys to the library. Dudley had foolishly expected to find rooms full of old newspapers, but instead there were rows of filing cabinets labelled for different states, and sub-divided into dailies, weeklies and occasional papers. Blumfeld remembered the name of the paper and the date Dudley had mentioned, without any need for reminder. He checked the files to make sure they had the paper, found the microfiche and put it in the machine.

Then while Dudley studied the microfiche through the magnifier, turning the handle to move slowly from page to page, Blumfeld busied himself at a telephone in another part of the office. When Dudley went over to him he was sitting on a chair, with his feet up on another. He dialled a number, held out the telephone. Dudley put it to his ear, and listened to a recorded message delivered in a flat, rather bored voice:

'The House of Usher will be open tonight in Soho at 8 Barkman Place, off West Broadway. Entrance is 75 dollars, the time ten p.m. The show lasts ninety minutes. Performers will include Madame Carbiche, Gerda Grateful and Tanya the Tiger Tamer. Audience participation is not encouraged. Thank you.'

'Did you get the stuff you wanted from the paper? You did, good. There you are, that's where the House is tonight.'

'Who are they, these performers?'

'Some amateurs, some professionals, dominatrixes, maybe a pair of lesbian wrestlers.'

'And what did they mean by saying audience participation is not encouraged?'

'Some of these shows are kind of orgies, everybody into everything. They're saying this is not like that. Course, it could be just to show the pigs they're respectable. You going?'

'I think so.'

'You look awful. Anything wrong?' Dudley shook his head. As a student Blumfeld had never shown interest in anybody but himself, but now he took his feet off the chair. 'You look like you had some sorta shock.'

'I have.'

'Something to do with the papers you were looking at, or —'

'The papers.'

'Yeah, well, you don't wanna believe what the papers say. Ask

175

me how do I know? I write 'em.' He shook briefly with laughter. 'Look, these House of Usher shows, I said they were mostly for tourists. So they are, but you wanna be careful.'

'I'll remember.'

'Most of 'em there are just nothing, never will be anything, but one or two — look, I got nothing special on tonight, you want me to come along? Mind you, I'm out of all that stuff and into nothing at all, but still they know me and I know them, through the mag and all that. So if you'd like me with you —'

There could be no doubt that Blumfeld was showing concern, and even something astonishingly like pity.

'It's good of you, but I think I should be on my own.'

'Suit yourself. Give Graham a kiss for me, and tell them there's one alumnus who'll never be back for Homecoming.'

What he noticed, what in particular he had not expected, was the smell, sweet and faintly sickly, a combination of pot and sex and something more, perhaps the smell of animal expectancy. He was in a large loft, one end of which had been converted into a rudimentary stage, with a platform and a curtain behind it. The loft was dark, something again which he had not expected, so that even if Annabel Lee was in the audience there was little hope of recognising her. A young man or woman — the sex was indeterminate — had taken his money, and another unisex figure had shown him up steep uncarpeted stairs and then to one of the wooden chairs which, with benches, served as seats. He looked about him but at first could see little in the gloom. As his eyes became accustomed to the lack of light he noticed groups of twos and threes close together on the benches. He was aware of a sniffing sound around his legs, the presence of a body. A head nuzzled his crotch. He struck down sharply, and was rewarded by a yelp.

'Bad manners, Fido. You'll have to be punished. He *will* go after people, he's not properly house-trained yet, I'm sorry.'

The speaker took the chair next to him. She was a woman, deep-voiced, her age uncertain in the darkness. She wore a skin-tight trouser suit in some light colour. Fido sank down at her feet. A chain went round his neck, and he yelped again as she pulled on it. Fido was a man whose age, like hers, was hard to determine, but he was not young, for the head he turned upwards to her in a pleading manner was almost bald.

'First time?'

'Yes.'

'I come every week. Tonight's special. I never miss Madame Carbiche, she gets me going. Like discipline?'

The words resembled so closely the question he had often

been asked at academic conferences, *What's your discipline?* that he was startled. 'I beg your pardon?'

'Like being disciplined?'

'I don't think so. No, certainly not.'

'Okay, okay.' She turned away from him, and Fido also shifted a few inches as though in disapproval. Torches glimmered here and there as the loft filled up. A Japanese man took the chair next to him, on the other side from Fido and his mistress, and produced a camera.

'Excuse me. Do you know if I may use camera?'

'I'm afraid I don't know.'

'At the hotel they say this is best show in New York. I am here from Japan, staying only four days, wish to see good show. This show very kinky, I am told.'

'Very likely, but I can't tell you. It's my first time here.'

'Mine also,' the Japanese said, and laughed heartily.

The loft was perhaps three-quarters full, with some forty people in it, when a man stepped from behind the curtain and was illuminated by a spotlight. He was tall and thin, with a pockmarked face. He wore a shirt with the Stars and Stripes on the front, and black and white striped trousers. His manner, and style of speech, recalled to Dudley a man introducing the turns at an old-time music hall.

'Ladies and gentlemen, welcome to the House of Usher, and the most sizzlingly sophisticated show the Big Apple can provide. We offer pulchritude in plenty, servitude with a smile, devilishly delightful domination. Our first presentation is the famous Madame Carbiche, who's carved them into hamburgers in Hamburg and aggravated their anguish in Amsterdam. Her very first show back in little old New York is at the House of Usher, where else? And she has two helpers, the lip-lickingly lovely Eve and adulatingly adorable Adam. Here she is.'

The Japanese raised his camera. At the first flash a voice near the door shouted: 'No pictures.'

Madam Carbiche came from behind the curtain. She was dressed in shiny black satin, and might have been any age between forty and sixty. Her arms were bare, except for black gloves up to the elbows. Her figure was magnificent, her face hawk-like with a beaky nose and spots of colour on the cheekbones, her manner contemptuous as she stood with hands on hips looking at the audience.

The sight of her was too much for the Japanese. His camera flashed again, once, twice. The voice now was just behind them.

'I said no pictures, bud. Gimme that camera.' The Japanese protested. 'Give it or get out. `All right, maybe you shoulda been told when you came in, but I'm saying it now, no pictures.' The Japanese passed over the camera. 'You get it back when the show's over.'

Madame Carbiche was talking. 'My name's Madame Carbiche. I'm a dominatrix, and in case you don't know what that means I'll tell you what I'd like to do to you out there. I'd put ropes right round your necks, a harness fixed so it's really tight and cuts where you'd know it, and then I'd have you crawling round my feet like the filthy disgusting creatures you are. You'd lick my feet, wash them with your tongues. Those who said no would get a taste of the whip. *And* you'd like it. Then —'

As Madame Carbiche elaborated on what she would like to do to them, Dudley was reminded of some English comedian of his youth, perhaps Max Miller, whose speciality had been insulting the audience. But the comedian's approach had been light-hearted, the sharing of a joke, where this was meant to be taken seriously. Beside him Fido was nuzzling his mistress, and Madame Carbiche herself was evidently excited by what she said. There was a sigh of approval as she told them that she would demonstrate her meaning with the help of Adam and Eve.

Adam and Eve were not more than twenty years old. They came on to the stage naked, and performed various sex acts with Madame Carbiche's encouragement, if that was the right word for the abuse she showered on them, the disgust she expressed for everything they did. The culmination of the act was her slow stripping by Eve, who then satisfied her sexually while she whipped Adam with a cat-o'-nine-tails, shrieking imprecations on them both throughout. The cat-o'-nine-tails, although wielded with apparent ferocity, left no marks. The whole thing was play-acting, of a most distasteful kind, but play-acting nonetheless. Dudley understood what Blumfeld had meant by calling the show a tourist trap.

The other scenes were play-acting too, whether it was Gerda Grateful accepting submissively and with apparent pleasure the humiliations to which she was subjected, or the three Veritable Vestal Virgins who were tied up by priests, naked except for their Cardinals' hats. The Virgins struggled vainly to escape from their bonds while the priests assaulted them. Their cries seemed to Dudley the best acting in the show. The woman with the dog went out, still with Fido on his chain. As the dog-man passed Dudley he growled, pretended to snap, and then giggled. The two were followed by another shadowy figure. Evidently Fido's mistress had found somebody else who liked to be disciplined.

After these turns Dudley's interest wandered. What had Garnish meant by saying that he might find Annabel Lee in the House of Usher? With eyes now accustomed to the semi-darkness he looked about him, but although there were women in the audience the few faces he could distinguish looked nothing like hers. The Japanese whispered, 'Very fine show, I think. I like very much.'

He quoted Garnish. 'There's a House of Usher in every big city.'

'I do not think we have one in Tokyo.'

The next turn involved some highly flexible Orientals, and at the end of it the Japanese clapped with particular enthusiasm. Then came Tanya the Tiger Tamer. Two cages were brought on to the stage, followed by men in tiger skins who showed long curved claws, and roared unconvincingly. After them, cracking her whip, wearing only thigh boots, Tanya appeared. The tigers advanced on her, snarling. She slashed at them with the whip, pointed to the cages. One tiger slunk in that direction, the other turned, jumped at her. They were on the ground in a flurry of tiger skin and flesh, with the other tiger joining in. Tanya emerged from it, blood apparently streaming from claw marks on arms and breasts. She hit them savagely with the whip, crying out unintelligible words in lust and anger.

It was the sound of the voice, even though he could not

distinguish the words, that told him. Strange, he thought afterwards, that recognition should have come through the voice, rather than by sight of the body he had known so well.

Tanya the Tigress was Annabel Lee.

He did not wait to see the end of the act, with its obligatory ritual of sex, but got up, pushed past the Japanese and others to the door, and went down the steep stairs. He crossed the road, leaned against a wall and took deep breaths, like a swimmer coming up from under water. Around him was the apparatus of the usual. The lights of a fast-food store and of the Orl Nite Koffee Shop shone no more than a few yards away. He knew that now he had found her at last he would not leave without talking to Annabel Lee, but had little idea what to say. He walked to the corner of Barkman Place, where it joined West Broadway, and back again, all the time taking those deep breaths.

People came out of the show. He looked at them curiously, finding nothing in their conventional appearance to suggest the nature of the performances they had watched. The Japanese passed, camera slung over his shoulder. There was a pair of obvious lesbians, and a group of half-a-dozen tourists, but most of the people who came down from the loft were men and women together, perhaps business executives and their wives or mistresses, out for an evening of sexually stirring entertainment. Fido and his mistress were evidently unusual.

'Hallo.'

He turned and saw Paul Race. 'Hallo.'

'You don't seem surprised to see me.'

'No. I worked out that the reason you looked shocked at the party was that you'd heard Garnish say she could be found here. Have you seen the show?' Race shook his head. 'You knew she was in it?'

'I guessed. She's been in it before, others too. I'd hoped —'

'You hoped she'd be on that flight to Johannesburg.'

Race did not reply, but continued to stare across the road at the narrow door leading up to the loft. Below was a factory, closed and shuttered. There seemed to Dudley nothing strange in the acceptance by them both of a knowledge neither had previously admitted, as though Annabel Lee was a link between them that made explanations needless. A woman came out with a man beside her, and when she asked the man to get a cab Dudley recognised the strident tones of Madame Carbiche. Otherwise he would not have known that commonplace figure wrapped in a shabby fur coat for the harpy who had shrieked obscenities at them all in the House of Usher.

Then she appeared, a man with her. Dudley felt Race stiffen beside him. Perhaps he stiffened similarly himself. They crossed the road together. She saw them before they reached her, and stopped beneath a street light. Her campanion stopped too. He was young, in his early twenties, slight, with fair hair and rabbit teeth.

'Well,' she said. 'Lee. Paul. A couple of Englishmen far from home. This is Jerry.'

At the sound of that light voice with its undercurrent of amusement and self-mockery, Dudley felt an uncomfortable tightening of the throat. It was difficult to speak, and the words that came out were far removed from any in his mind. 'I suppose Jerry is one of your tigers.'

'You saw the show,' she said, with the pleasure of one making a first appearance on Broadway or at the National Theatre. 'Did you like it?'

He was saved from reply by Paul Race. He spoke words familiar to Dudley from many a bad film, and it was with a sensation of unreality that he heard them spoken now. They seemed an extension of the play-acting he had been watching.

'Lee, I have to talk to you.'

'Oh dear, have you? Jerry, you'd better run along.'

Rabbit teeth said fiercely, 'If you want me, I'll stay.'

Again amusement rippled. 'Thank you, Jerry, but they're both old friends.'

'If you say so. 'Night then, Lee, you were wonderful.' With the same feeling of watching a play Dudley saw him snatch her hand and kiss it before walking away.

She looked from one to the other of them, then spoke to Dudley. 'I suppose you want to talk to me as well. Now you've caught up. Why don't we all go along the road and say hallo over a hamburger? I'm hungry.' He remembered that she was always hungry after the act. 'The Orl Nite is nice and handy. They know me.' When Paul began to protest she cut him short. 'That's the way we're going to talk, if it's talk you want. No heart-to-hearts.'

The Orl Nite Koffee Shop was like a thousand others. They sat at a plastic-topped table, she on one side, the two of them on the other, Race beside the wall. It was nearly midnight and there were few customers, but the girl who took the order looked as fresh as she no doubt had been at midday. Annabel Lee ordered a jumbo hamburger with chips, and onion rings on the side. Dudley, suddenly aware of hunger himself, asked for a pastrami on rye. Paul said that he would only have coffee. In what seemed no time the food was on the table.

'There you go,' the girl said as she put it down. 'Enjoy your meal.' She gave Paul a smile that flicked on and off like a camera shutter. 'Enjoy your coffee.'

She spread mustard on her hamburger, injected it with tomato sauce, bit. 'M-m,' she said appreciatively, then looked expectantly from one to the other of them, a schoolgirl hoping for a treat.

'You were supposed to take that flight to Johannesburg,' Paul Race said. 'You swore you'd never come back here.'

'I changed my mind. I like it here. Feels like home.'

'Lee,' Paul said imploringly. It seemed the moment for Dudley to speak.

'That isn't your name. Not Annabel Lee but Lenore. You're Lenore Fetherby.'

'Not the scatty sister, the wicked one.' She licked tomato sauce off her fingers. 'How do you make that out? Lenore burned up in a fire.'

'No. I checked the file of the El Paso paper.'

She made a face. 'Real old bloodhound, aren't you? Professor Potter on the trail.'

'That was when I understood the whole thing. Shall I tell you what happened? I can't prove all of it, but enough to be sure of what you did.'

She speared an onion ring. 'Why not? This place stays

183

open all night.' She shook her head at Paul Race. 'Let the man talk.'

He had thought about it so much, had had so many glimpses of the truth, that now it all came out orderly and fluent. 'It must have begun with your mother's funeral. You turned up expecting to get half the money if you were lucky, something anyway, and there was nothing at all. Your mother thought you were a bad influence on Annie, but I believe there was more than that. Some of those pictures she painted that were hanging in the house she called The Kingdom by the Sea show a woman running away from a figure without a face. I believe you were that figure, she had you in mind. She was afraid of you.'

'She might have been worried about Lenore. I told you she was a bad lot, ran away from home, got sent to Borstal, swanned around with some dicey Arab businessmen.'

'Yes, you told me. That was frank of you.'

'But I'm not Lenore, I'm Lee. Anything else is your imgination.'

He said patiently, 'Very well, I'll talk in the third person. At the funeral Lenore met Paul Race for the first time. Your uncle Stewart said she took the news very well, wished her sister joy of the money, and said she'd be taking the first train out of Halifax. I think she went back to London with Paul — either he was on the train or he gave her a lift in his car — and the idea crossed her mind then. In five years' time Annabel Lee would be thirty, and come into her inheritance. But suppose she wasn't there, might it be possible for Lenore to take her place? At that time it was no more than an idea. I daresay she had other possibilities in mind, one of those rich Arabs perhaps.'

She made a face at him, laughing. On the other side of the table she shone, she positively sparkled, carefree as he had ever known her. Then Race muttered, 'We came back in my car,' and the look she gave him was that of Tanya the Tiger Tamer.

'But the rich Arabs lost their money, or got tired of her, or she got tired of them, and some time last year she did the indispensable thing, took the step necessary to make the plan work. She went to bed with Paul Race, I don't know

184

just when —'

'August,' Race said in a flat, weary voice. 'We met in August. She rang me at the office, said she was in London, asked if we could meet.'

'And within a few days Lenore was telling him the plan.'

He paused, but Race said no more.

'It wasn't such an outrageous idea as it might sound, because it's true that Annabel Lee had always been fairly scatty. The nearest thing she had to a permanent home was a flat in London, but she was often away from it for weeks or even months at a time. She did as she pleased, took jobs here and there especially with little theatre companies, sometimes stayed in the house up at Scarness. She had no set pattern of life, no close friends. The two of you resembled each other, had similar features, although anybody who knew Annabel Lee at all well, like the woman in the flat below at Kennington, would have known the difference at once.

'But suppose Annabel Lee was out of Britain when the time came for her to inherit and decided to stay away, said she'd had enough of English life, nobody would think it very strange. There was just one thing.' He put a hand on Race's arm. The other shivered as though the touch had given him an electric shock. 'She had to have somebody who'd swear to her. He would have to go to Johannesburg or Montevideo or wherever she might be, and say, "Yes, I know her, this is Annabel Lee Fetherby". It had to be somebody whose word would be accepted. And the somebody was you. For you to go along with such a scheme you'd need to be well and truly hooked, but she managed that. She'd hooked a good many in her time.'

Race sighed, and said simply 'Yes.' She shook her head at him, smiling.

'You were the indispensable man. Steve knew Annabel Lee and would have seen through a deception at once, but he was occupied with his own publishing problems. He'd have been only too happy for his right-hand man to take a trip abroad and identify her. After all, you knew her too. So you were to authenticate Lenore as being Annabel Lee. She got the money, you resigned your job — you'd prepared the ground for that — and the two of you lived happily ever after in Paraguay or Ecuador or Argentina. That was the idea, wasn't it, Race?'

The young man had moved as far away from Dudley as possible, pressing into the corner of the seat. His face also was turned away. His neat profile was pale.

She asked: 'What happened to Annabel Lee?'

'Lenore made a date to see her at The Kingdom by the Sea in October, probably appealing for a hand-out. She went to Yorkshire, there was a fight, she killed her sister or more likely knocked her unconscious. Mrs Waddington told me she found things broken, and had never known anything like it to happen before. She was going to give Miss Fetherby a piece of her mind the next time she saw her, and say she should clear up her own breakages. But she never did see Annabel Lee again. She was dead.'

'I asked before, in this tale what happened to her?'

'I'd say Lenore pushed her over the cliff. I'm sure she was on her own, Race would have had nothing to do with it. She may have stripped the body first, she may have rendered it unrecognisable, I wouldn't put anything past her. And she was lucky. Mrs Waddington told me there'd been a body washed up some time in November, twenty miles north of Scarness. It was unidentifiable, but there'd been a girl disappeared locally, from Whitley Bay, a few months earlier, and the police assumed it was her. I believe it was Annabel Lee. That was when she died.'

'You believe,' she said ironically. She finished the hamburger, sighed with pleasure. 'Is that all?'

'It's the background, and I can't prove it. It's also where I come in.'

'Do you now? I was wondering when that would happen. Let's hear that, let's hear the rest of it.' She smiled at Race, who responded by looking down at the table top. 'But I'd like some more coffee.'

She gestured to the girl, who brought over the jug, poured coffee. The two men shook their heads. She's enjoying it, Dudley thought, I'll swear she's enjoying it all.

'This was in October, and it left time to be filled in. I don't know whose bright idea it was to establish positively that

Annabel Lee was still alive after October, but it was obviously unwise for her to stay around in England. An identification by somebody other than Race would be useful, so somebody had the idea that Lenore might come up to Graham to fool me. Then I'd be another witness to the existence of Annabel Lee.'

'It was my idea.' Now Race turned to face him, the pretty features pinched, the face a little green. 'Steve talked about you often, made you sound like somebody who'd believe anything you werc told. The idea was that you'd be corroboration. If Steve asked when Annabel Lee left England and where had she been, it would turn out his oldest friend had met her at Graham, talked to her. But it was never meant — I never imagined —'

'That I'd be hooked too, like you and goodness knows how many others. But Lenore always dangles the line for the fish. She likes her fun, you should have known that.'

She said, 'And wasn't it fun for you too?'

'You are Lenore. You admit it.'

'Oh my, how you like to see all the sticks laid out straight. Okay, for the purpose of this conversation I'm Lenore.'

He acknowledged this with a nod. 'It was at Graham that things went wrong, when Annabel Lee's ex-husband, whom neither you nor many other people knew to exist, turned up there. No wonder he looked surprised when he was told you were Annabel Lee, he had the best of reasons for knowing you weren't. It must have been a shock, but you take things as they come. You went back to England with him, left a note saying goodbye to the poor hooked fish at Graham. I don't know what you told Wolfdale, but you hooked him as easily as the rest of us. He thought he'd found a playmate, but to you he was just somebody who had to be kept quiet. When he found your air ticket for Johannesburg and wanted to know what you were playing at, you had a row which ended up with you shooting him. Was it your revolver?'

'The funny thing was, it was his. I asked if I could look at it and, do you know, he gave it me.' She shook her head at the foolishness of people.

'And you shot him?'

'No, it wasn't like that. He thought he could move in, take

possession, and I don't like that, never did. He fairly blew up when he found the air ticket, and it just so happened I'd still got the revolver. We had a terrible argument, and then — it was kind of an accident really.'

'I don't think so. You'd never have left yourself dancing to his tune. And you would have been, because he knew you weren't Annabel Lee, he'd have wanted a cut when he knew what you were trying to do. I think you just got the revolver and shot him.'

'Think what you like.'

'But there was something else you hadn't reckoned on, your hooked fish from Graham being pulled all the way across the Atlantic, sure you were in great trouble, trying to find you. When you learned I was in England you must have planned with Paul here to put me off the track. Paul led me down to Islington where some girl you knew established that Annabel Lee was alive because she'd stayed a night in the girl's apartment, and showed me a cutting saying Lenore was dead, just in case I should get any other idea. Then when I went up to Yorkshire you made a recording and it was played to me on the 'phone, with you telling me to give up looking for you. That was a mistake, because when I thought about it, who knew I was going to visit The Kingdom by the Sea that day, and that I'd be there to receive a call? Only Paul. It was then I first thought you two might be partners.

'There were all sorts of things that should have put me on the track, the way you made sure you weren't seen by Mrs Morris when you left, the fact that you wrote a letter to Crundall telling him to clear out the flat instead of doing it in person. Of course he'd met your sister in local pubs, he'd have known at once that you weren't the same person. That letter should have told me the truth at once. Then you used to swim with me at Graham, and as I learned in Yorkshire, Annabel Lee couldn't swim. There was the mess you made of trying to cook some of her recipes. You felt you had to try, because Annabel Lee had written the cookery book and it might seem odd if you didn't try to cook. Yet it still seemed to me that you couldn't be Lenore, because I knew she was dead. I had a wild idea that somebody might be pursuing you both, and had burnt Lenore to death in El Paso. At least I had that idea until tonight, when I looked up the story in the El Paso paper, and found it didn't exist, never happened. You'd just had a bit of type set up, and arranged for that girl to plant it on me.'

There was no change in her bright smiling. 'It was Paul's idea, like the one about making the tape. A lot of his ideas sounded good. Trouble was, they didn't work. Is that all?'

'Isn't it enough?'

'I've enjoyed listening to you, I can see what keeps your students on the edge of their chairs, but it's only a story, all talk.'

'Steve would know in a moment that you're not Annabel Lee.'

'My dear sweet Dud, I'm not going back to the mother country.'

'But I shall write to Steve, and if you try to claim from abroad —'

'Of course I can't claim, I know it. It was all a bright idea, I do really still think it was, but it went wrong. When something goes wrong it's a pity, but you don't cry about it, you give up and start thinking about something else. I shan't claim any money, that's well and truly scuppered. But you can't prove any of the things you've been saying, and if you could I don't suppose you'd try. You wouldn't want innocent Annabel Lee to suffer, would you, not even if her name's Lenore and she's not so innocent. So, boys, I'm going back to the crummy joint I call home at the moment, and I suggest you do likewise.'

'There's something I want to know,' Paul said.

'Any little thing.'

'That air ticket. Who tore it up?'

'Why, I did. Ira found it, and he got so het up, I thought I'd better.'

'You could have got a replacement, you could have gone out there. It was what we'd agreed, that you'd go out and wait there until June, then I'd validate the inheritance and join you. You knew I hated all this, I didn't want you back here.' She smiled at him, said nothing. 'You never meant to go to Johannesburg, did you?'

'Since you ask, no. Jo'burg's nice but provincial.' She spread her arms wide. 'This is home.'

'When you'd got the money you'd have left me.'

Still smiling she said, 'Since there's no money, what does it matter?'

'Apple pie.' The waitress bore a tray on which were three silver-wrapped packets on plates. She put them down, and removed the wrappings to reveal pastry. 'Aunt Mary's Apple Pie, specialty of the house.'

'But we didn't order it,' Dudley said.

'Every customer gets one, our compliments. It's a celebration. The Orl Nite opened a year ago today.'

'Apple pie,' she said joyfully. She had risen from her seat but now sat down again. They were the last words she spoke.

The waitress put her hand over her mouth. She was looking at Paul Race.

He held a tiny revolver, the little nozzle blueish, the butt mother-of-pearl. Dudley began to say something. He could never remember what the words had been.

'It was my mother's,' Paul said. 'She kept it beside the bed to frighten burglars.'

He fired. There was little noise, no more than from a cap revolver.

The waitress screamed, and dropped her tray.

A darker colour appeared on the blue shirt. The expression on the face above the shirt, joyfully expectant, eager for pleasure, did not change.

Dudley leaned over to grasp Paul's right hand which held the revolver, but succeeded only in jogging his arm. The second shot made a small hole in the forehead. Then there was another, much louder explosion, which seemed to be in Dudley's ear.

A man came round from behind the serving counter wiping his hands. The waitress screamed and screamed.

Paul's head dropped on to Dudley's shoulder. He put up his hand to push it away, and the hand came away bloody. The head dropped to the table. Blood gushed from the mouth on to the plastic table top.

The girl still sat on the opposite side of the table, with the little hole in her forehead and the widening stain on her shirt. She looked serene. This was the death of Lenore Fetherby, but the second death of Annabel Lee. Looking at her, Dudley remembered the lines she had spoken to him with pleasure, as it seemed very long ago:

Never Mark Antony
Dallied more wantonly
With the fair Egyptian Queen.